THE SUM OF HIS SYNDROMES

The Sum of His Syndromes

A NOVEL

K. B. Dixon

ACADEMY

CHICAGO

Published in 2009 by
Academy Chicago Publishers
363 West Erie Street
Chicago, Illinois 60654

© 2009 by K. B. Dixon

A portion of this book originally appeared in *Open Spaces Magazine*.
Printed in the U.S.A.

Library of Congress Cataloging-in-Publication
on file with the publisher.

As always, for Sandra Jean

ONE

It's 8:45 a.m. and I have locked myself in the third stall of the sixth-floor men's room—the one nearest the wall. I am sitting exactly where you would expect me to be sitting, scribbling away in a buff-colored steno pad stolen specifically for the occasion. I've been spending more and more time in here lately because I can't keep spending it out there. Out there it's telephones and computers and all sorts of people with problems, people who want to interrupt what you are doing (or not doing), people who want to talk to you, people who want to tell you things you're not interested in hearing. People like Robert Bray, for example, who knows everything there is to know about the downtown condo market, and Lucy McAllister, who seems to think your life would be improved if you knew more guys named Cooter.

*

Had an interesting session with Dr. Costa yesterday. He wanted to focus on the negative feelings I seem to have toward Mrs. Dorton, the evil manageress of my apartment building. I told him my negative feelings for her were mostly in response to her negative feelings toward me, but, as always, he seems reluctant to accept what I am telling him as true.

He has an interesting theory. He thinks I have focused my attention on her as a way of not focusing it on myself, that my unhappiness with my unhappiness is driving me to see her as some sort of persecutor when, in fact, it's just me trying to avoid admitting things to myself—namely, that I have an inclination to romanticize what (for want of a less loaded word) we have tentatively agreed to call my "depression" and that this inclination is predicated on a quaint eighteenth-century belief in the sanctity of a certain sort of suffering.

A wiry, wedge-headed guy in his middle 40s, Dr. C looks like he could be, is, or has been at one time, a runner. He is the third guy I've seen in the last three years. Calm, quiet, quick to write prescriptions—I can't help feeling he is dangerous.

★

Dean Freeze was just in here working on his teeth. He was flossing, brushing, mouth-washing. There is a scrupulousness about him that is sort of mesmerizing. He never seems to have a hair out of place. It just doesn't seem possible that a person could be that clean and spotless.

★

There is a rumor floating around that Cathy Manning's daughter attacked a neighbor kid with a bat.

★

I have a strong feeling that Kate doesn't really want to meet Peter. She has heard things about him—about the extremity of his personality—and he doesn't sound to her like someone she would like very much, which worries her. It worries her because she knows how much I like him, and she has no idea what her not liking him might mean for us. We were cubicle mates, Peter and I, for three years—until he inherited some walking-away money from a dying grandmother.

I think Kate is also worried about the *way* she might not like Peter. She is not the sort of person who would think more of someone because of someone they knew, but she is the sort who might think less. At this point in our relationship she seems to want to think as much of me as she can, and she is afraid Peter might interfere with this. That I'm the sort of person who would know someone like him might end up being a hurdle too high to get over. It would mean something—exactly what, at this moment anyway, is a mystery.

⋆

I'm not as interested as I should be in wanting to make an impression on Dr. C. So far he doesn't seem to have noticed this because he's been busy trying to make an impression on me. He wants me to find him even-tempered and caring. Once I do that, we can begin our work in earnest.

⋆

Paul Burkholder is just back from his vacation. He spent a month walking across Montana. He's been regaling us with stories that are basically about what a brave and adventurous guy he is. Everyone he ran into along the way seems to have been amazed that he was doing what he was doing.

⋆

Excerpt from a conversation between Bruce Howland and Ryan Brown:

"It doesn't seem like I'm laughing as much as I used to. It's not like I'm getting serious; I just don't seem to know what's funny anymore."

"You might try looking at your tie."

*

Had a long lunchtime conversation with Peter about Jennifer Rasmussen, a girl who used to work here. He got an email from her catching him up on things—trips to the beach, barbecues, visits to the butterfly exhibition at the zoo—and he was in a flap trying to decide if he should send her a copy of *Cubicle Dreams*, a collection of short stories he had just finished publishing. On one hand he wanted to send her a copy because she was in school now and surrounded (presumably) by people who read, and he was hoping she might feel inclined to encourage a few of them to buy it; on the other, he was reluctant because of a passage in one of the stories in which he said something not especially nice about her.

The story in question—a fragmented, not particularly successful look at a week in the life of an office drudge he calls Daniel—is clearly autobiographical. The offending passage involved a description of this Daniel's reaction to his new officemate, a guy named Gary. He describes Gary as being inherently more entertaining, thoughtful, and interested in things than the officemate just departed—someone who, in spite of having her name and hair color changed and being sent to nursing rather than dental school, was still pretty clearly Jennifer. Peter could imagine her reading the section and feeling betrayed or hurt, and he didn't want that. He knew the chances of her finding the paragraph were small because even though she read, she did not as a rule read the sort of stuff he wrote, and the passage at issue—the not-as-entertaining, thoughtful, or interested passage—was about a third of the way into the book, behind the infamously alienating story number 5. If she did actually start the book, it wasn't likely she would get to the scene of the crime. But still. . . .

★

Dr. C says I'm a fine person and it's his job to make me realize that. I've tried to make it clear to him that I'm not one of those patients who insist on his opinions being favorable or his forecasts optimistic.

★

You never want to talk to Steven Pounder first thing in the morning. He drives in from Forest Grove and the traffic on Highway 26 is just too much for him. It takes an hour at least for him to regain his pre-commute sense of humor.

★

The light in here is worse than the light out there. The light out there makes you look tired; the light in here makes you look ill.

★

Excerpt from a conversation between Stewart McKinney and Doug Arrington:

"The babysitter makes me nervous. She is nice enough, but she forgot to give Rachael her medicine before she went to bed—the stuff for her ear infection. Also, I think she goes through our things when we're gone. I think she knows how much I've got in my retirement account."

★

I understand Kate's trepidation. On paper Peter doesn't look all that good—an isolated introvert with an inclination to be remote and caustic. But he has things going for him—valuable things—and I think she'll see that. He is smart and funny, and behind that remoteness and hostility, there is a heart. It's a strong friendship, but probably not as strong as she thinks. It's predicated on our previous proximity, our mutual interests, and the fact that when he used to work here I felt distinctly less conspicuous.

In some ways it seems to me that he is the person I might have been if it weren't for certain civilizing influences.

*

The word is out there, I know. I can feel it in the interoffice wind. I wonder what will be left of me.

*

Gail Swearingen is known for always leaving the Xmas party early to go home and walk her dog. I understand the dilemma, and I commiserate. I think she has been unfairly stigmatized. Toby and his beagle-sized bladder have cut all sorts of evenings short for me. Peculiar—the things we allow to control our lives.

*

We haven't been seeing each other all that long, but I think already Kate is starting to trust me. If I say I'm going to call around such and such a time, I call around such and such a time. If I say I'll come over, I come over. It simply wouldn't occur to me not to. She seemed surprised at first at this sort of unvarying fidelity. I don't want to guess why.

*

Peter published his story collection using one of the new on-demand-publishing services. He says it was emancipating and he couldn't imagine ever wanting to do it any other way.

*

I am a little suspicious of Dr. C's attitude toward depression. It seems to go beyond what you would expect given the nature of his occupation. I have a strong feeling it is, in part, because he himself is not now, nor has he ever been, a depressive, and he resents the privileged way depressives seem to be thought of in the general culture. He is, I think, especially envious of claims to special knowledge. As a non-depressive, he thinks he has been undervalued. He'd like to see us interpret depression differently. If we did, we would interpret him differently. We would see him more the way he wants to be seen, more the way he sees himself—as a smart and serious man who is the equal of almost any gloomy genius.

*

Right now Peter is working on a novel titled *The 34-Pound Dog*. Basically it's about me and the aforementioned evil manageress, Margaret Dorton. She and I have never gotten along very well, but we went through a particularly rough patch a couple of years ago. There was a time when I was convinced she had started sneaking into my apartment to feed Toby (the idea being to get him up over 35 pounds, the maximum weight allowed in my lease, and then hand me over to the lawyers). It's this particular period that Peter is focusing on. He says he has an idea of how it is going to end, but for right now he is keeping it to himself.

*

Kate doesn't quite disapprove of the amount I drink, but she comes close to it. If I drank just a little more it would be something we would have to talk about. I would have to make myself conscious of my consumption—especially when we were out with other people where it's so easy to lose track.

★

I know from time to time she has been tempted to understand certain of my peculiarities as cultivated, but she has not given in to that temptation and for that I am grateful. If I were in her place I probably would have written me off as a self-indulgent twit a long time ago.

★

Basically I see Dr. C to assure Kate that I am not afraid to learn too much. I think this is the only thing I am currently deceiving her about.

★

Pam at one of the lunchroom vending machines:
"Jeeze, Sandra, you picked your husband faster than you're picking that sandwich."

★

Peter has a veritable stable of hobbyhorses. He was riding one of his favorites last night—book editors and the surreptitious role they play in the production of certain texts. The more he learned about the way traditional publishing works, the more he felt it imperative to publish himself. He didn't have the energy, he said, to argue with all of that savvy.

★

Linda Marshall has a terrible smile. It's very disorienting. It looks more like a grimace than anything—like she has just tasted something sour. She is always looking for someone to confide in. It took her about a month to figure out it wasn't going to be me.

★

I'm tense. I'm nervous. I'm on edge. I feel like I'm standing in the wrong line.

★

I knew right away that Kate was going to be someone important to me because right away I was worried about how I acted toward her. Normally, I don't worry about that sort of thing very much. I think or feel one way and if someone for some reason misinterprets that, I don't especially care—unless, of course, it is a significant misinterpretation, one that causes problems or discomfort for those involved. Insignificant misinterpretations mean little to me—except when Kate is involved. I don't want there to be any misunderstandings between us—no matter how trivial.

★

Noel Evans has had two concussions—one when his wife hit him in the head with a bottle of champagne, the other when she hit him in the head with a lamp.

★

Dr. C has a tendency to view intuitive insight as hallucinatory.

★

Kate has tried several times to figure out just exactly when she fell in love with me. She thinks there is just such a moment, but she's confused about when it might have been. All she knows for sure is that it happened. She thinks if she could put her finger on just when it happened she would be able to understand it a little better, and if she understood it a little better, she could do something about it when she needed to—like right now, for instance.

It perturbs her that I am not similarly interested in the exact moment I realized my feelings for her. I remember the first time

I told her I loved her, but that is not quite the same thing. When exactly I fell in love with her or knew I was in love with her, I couldn't say. One week I wasn't and the next I was—that's the best I can do. It's not very romantic, I know, but my life is like that. It's full of moments that have sneaked up on me.

*

A suggestion here, a comment there—Dr. C tries in subtle ways to alter my understanding. He wants me to see certain attitudes of mine as symptoms—things to be treated medically like a rash.

*

Excerpt from a conversation between John Blake and Chris Young:

"I don't know, I feel like I'm sleepwalking."

"Me too. I'm trying not to wake myself up because I know I'm not going to be happy when I find out where I am."

*

Greg Linstrom has no idea what he expected his life to be like so he is not surprised to find out this is it. Nothing worries him. Nothing keeps him up at night. I don't understand him at all.

*

If Kate seems reluctant to meet Peter, he seems reluctant to meet her. I think he is afraid if he does, she'll become a part of our regular conversations.

*

I think you would have to say Arthur Valle is on the dweeby side. Gangly, pencil-necked, bespectacled—he looks like someone who was destined from an early age to be president of the chess club.

★

Dr. C doesn't really seem to understand that I am not proud of feeling the way I do. I don't believe these low moods are in themselves ennobling, but I do believe they are related to perspective and to the accuracy of one's perceptions of reality. I do believe they are related, however unfortunately, to what matters most at the end of the day.

★

There are few things in this world that smell better than breakfast.

★

Kate has simply stunning posture.

★

My left pocket is always full of Kleenex.

★

Some people will say anything. I try not to be one of them.

★

Interesting session. Told Dr. C I was reluctant to move on with Kate (if I can move on) because this is the beginning, which is almost always the best part. When it stops, there will be the middle, which has its moments but will always be something less because it is the middle, which means, in another sense, it's the beginning—the beginning of the end.

★

Maybe between the two of us we can trick me into being honest with you.

TWO

This venue leaves a lot to be desired. For instance, there are times like these when Delaney makes a visit. I don't want to be disgusting, but what does this guy eat for breakfast? Where is his sense of shame? Large, pot-bellied—he carries himself around the office like a pasha. One look at him and you know he is capable of anything in here. I know I'm supposed to admire his lack of inhibition, but I don't. Maybe I should bring this up with Dr. C.

*

Danita Gorski dyes her own hair.

*

The first time I saw Kate was in Dr. Hinkle's office. She was sitting behind a shiny walnut desk wearing a tight yellow sweater with some sort of hieroglyphic design crocheted around the neck. She glowed like something radioactive. I was referred to Dr. Hinkle by Dr. Lindsey, my first doctor—a mustachioed glad-hander who I had decided to leave for the usual reasons. Kate was one of three secretary/receptionists. (She worked for Hinkle; Lisa, her hideous friend—the one who is so set against me—worked for Dr. Bickling; and Teresa worked for Dr. Jaggar.)

*

There are a lot of people around here who make me feel lucky. Why can't I do something with that?

*

I don't remember how many sessions I had with Dr. Hinkle before I asked Kate to slip out and get a cup of coffee with me— I'm guessing maybe five or six. She said no, but she said it nicely. She said she was sure I would understand, but there was a strict policy in place forbidding the staff from socializing with patients.

Kate saying no is what led me to see Dr. Costa. When I left Dr. Lindsey I had a list of names. Dr Hinkle was at the top. I don't remember why. Next on the list was Dr. C.

I left Dr. Hinkle so I would no longer be a patient and officially banned from seeing Kate. I didn't tell Dr. C about this. In fact, I didn't mention Dr. Hinkle at all. I said I had been referred by Dr. Lindsey (renewing that unwanted association). When Dr. C asked why I had waited so long to get in touch, I lied. I said I had been feeling a little better and that I had wanted to see if I could handle things on my own for a while—regain a little self-respect. I said it hadn't worked out; I couldn't handle it—not in a manner I found acceptably mature anyway. I said I was here now in part because I found myself at the front end of a relationship that was worrying me, one I valued but expected to deteriorate because in my experience that seemed to be the nature of relationships. He asked about how I met Kate, so, of course, I had to cobble together another little lie.

★

There are important jobs in this unimportant department, but I don't have one of them. I have a low-level, paper-shuffling one. Certain people in positions of power expect me to have aspirations to positions of power like their own, but I don't. I have been careful not to let them know because if they knew they'd write me off, and if they wrote me off, there would be no reason for people in positions of lesser power not to write me off as well, which would mean the work that came my way would get steadily less endurable.

★

Elliott Hammond is the sort of guy you'd expect to have had one of those "funny" uncles. You know he has a story about visiting and at some point being touched.

★

I agree. There are lots of things I don't understand about myself. There are lots of things I don't understand about people in general. For example, I don't understand people who are courageous or people who like getting up early in the morning.

★

Jack Griffin thinks he is just a purchase away from being happy—in this instance, the purchase of a German sports car.

★

Excerpt from conversation between John Morris and Alex Kline:
"I'll never forget the first time I saw my grandmother take out her teeth."

*

Peter wished he had taken a little more time, but he had never really intended to publish a collection of stories—not now, not actually ever. It just sort of happened. It was a thing that developed a life and a momentum of its own—an accident brought on by a harmonic convergence of half-formed ideas. Among Peter's complaints: too many guys named Steven, too many women named Teresa, too many dogs, too many conspicuous words that should not have been repeated ("boneless" and "calibrated," for example).

*

The walls of my cubicle are forehead-high and covered with a fine-weave, elephant-gray, sound-absorbing burlap.

*

Yes, I like being liked, but it isn't important to me beyond a certain point (say, much beyond being liked by Kate). Of course I don't like being disliked, but similarly it isn't important to me unless there are real consequences (say, being disliked by David Gorman, one of my many supervisors). In most instances, I'm perfectly happy being ignored.

*

Excerpt from a conversation between Duane Moore and Larry Winters:

"For a while I hated pink, but there were so many shades of pink to hate I figured why bother. Now I hate turquoise."

*

I suppose the thing I wanted most when I walked through that door was for you to hold off a bit on your interpretation of me.

It seemed if I was serious about this, then being understood was going to be important and being understood was going to take some time. I didn't want to start negotiating the ultimate explanation with you right away. I wanted our positions to reveal themselves slowly, organically.

*

Robert Hoff is an inveterate watcher of the History Channel. He always has something to say about World War II.

*

How can I help you—that is supposed to be my official attitude. I can almost never manage it.

*

Dr. C wants me to know that he gets it—the world is devoid of meaning, and awareness of this is bound to affect one's mood. But he doesn't really get it—not much beyond saying so.

*

If I do this job the way it is supposed to be done I won't be able to do it very long, so I do it the way I'm doing it, which is a substandard way, hoping to prolong my time in it because, while I hate it, I'm sure any other job would be worse. I'm trying to keep from getting involved in one of those downward spirals that lead to who knows where.

*

Like most in his profession, Dr. C is very much afraid of suicides. They represent an appalling sort of personal failure. It is probably why he is so quick to prescribe.

*

I went to the dentist yesterday. I had to have two fillings replaced, and, yes, it was unpleasant—unusually so because they were putting in a different type of filling, one that takes a lot longer to do, and they were putting them in places that were hard to get at. I had to sit there for two hours with my mouth stretched open—with drilling and filling and other things going on, things that made it impossible to swallow. There was all sorts of equipment involved—clamps and hoses and air guns and terrible-tasting chemical things. The smell of burnt tooth enamel made my eyes water. Now I find it hurts when I chew on the new filling side—a sharp, needle-like pain shoots up the front of my face and into my eye. I called to see if this was something I should expect or if maybe something had gone wrong. Of course I couldn't talk to the dentist—he was busy torturing someone else—so the billing lady, an officious termagant named Judy, asked me a bunch of questions and told me she would have Joyce, his royal highness's assistant, call me, which she did.

I don't like Joyce because she talks to me like I am about eight. I don't know if this is just her manner or if she's singling me out for this patronization. She said the fillings probably needed adjusting, that I should come back in, that it wouldn't take long. I told her I was sorry but if it wasn't some sort of emergency then I wasn't coming back in for a while—not after the ordeal of having it done in the first place. I'd just have to live with it—I'd learn to chew on the left. I would get them adjusted when I had to come back in for a cleaning—which, by my calculations, would be a helluva long while from now.

*

Kate has started feeding me fish. She orders it when we go out, and she asks me to do the same. She thinks it will be good for my brain.

*

Randal Mahr works about a half-dozen cubicles from me. He is always stopping Craig Meilinger in the hall for a quick couple of words. They are buddies for no other reason than that they are gay—otherwise, they couldn't be less alike. Craig is young and immaculately dressed. He shaves and polishes his head. He is fast-walking, fast-talking, fast-thinking. Randal is none of these things.

*

Peter's stories don't look or feel like other stories. It probably means there is something wrong with them.

*

Kate worries, I think. If she is concerned about me being the sort of person who knows someone like Peter, what should she think of herself being someone who knows someone like me? What is being said about her here? Perhaps there is something wrong—something she has managed to stay unaware of. Why doesn't she seem to value greater solidity? Maybe she doesn't think she deserves any better. Maybe she's a masochist.

*

Darleen Weiss has told me several times now that if I adjust my chair just so, I can get myself ergonomically aligned, and if I can get myself ergonomically aligned, I can work without discomfort.

*

Peter was reading a story the other day about a writer who had his book pulled by his publisher at the last minute because they were afraid they might be sued for libel. He found it unbelievably depressing—not the story about the book being pulled, but the story about the book being written. The author, let's call him X, was complaining that he had no idea his publisher was worried about liability issues, that these worries had never come up in all of the work he had done with his editor—work he described. He said that so and so, the editor, had suggested he cut this character and that character and bring yet another character to the fore. He wanted X to make the story more dramatic—give it a stronger narrative through-line. X would send this editor pages, and this editor would send them back with notes. To Peter, that was not an editor—that was a co-author. He said if he wanted to get involved in collaborative work he'd get involved in movies where there was money and glamour and fun—not literary fiction where there was only poverty, misunderstanding, and heartbreak.

*

Excerpt of conversation between Keith Lazier and Alan Wallace: "I don't know—dance class? Does that strike you as something I should be sending my five-year-old son to?"

*

I would be more popular if I felt differently—and if I felt differently, I would probably care.

*

I overheard Aaron Anderson complaining to Terry Fitzsimmons about the lack of female companionship in his life. He said he thought that it might, in part, have something to do with the time of year, but he had been, as he put it, on his own for a few months now—ever since the divorce. He told Terry that he had started reading the personal ads, but he was having trouble getting into it because he found them so dispiriting. I took a look in the back of *Westside Watch*, the local alternative weekly. I see what he means. I found a woman who was trustworthy, enjoyed people, and loved the earth. Another who wanted someone she could talk with about her golf game. Still another wanted someone who put Jesus first. An appalling number said they liked camping—the clear implication being that you should too. Several women were looking for a soulmate. Does this word really mean anything to the people using it or is it just code—a way of saying they are looking for something that is not entirely about sex.

Of course as you read these things you can't help but start to wonder what your own ad might look like.

"Underachieving, low-paid, nonprofessional cog in relatively uncaring machine who is closer to being short than tall. A non-smoking occasional drinker with a sense of humor who likes good conversation, but has a short attention span. Not especially stable, but can cook better than most. Scored abysmally on standard 5 Factor Personality Test—i.e., a worried, hypercritical loner with an attenuated taste for the novel. Likes television, travel, movies, and books, but is by most accounts a picky elitist. Likes the beach, but has mixed feelings about the mountains. Cats no. Dogs yes. Hates dancing and would consider camping only in the case of a national emergency. Doesn't play the guitar, but can swim. No arrests (as an adult). No tattoos. Has never been to Aspen. Thinks sushi is for seals. Envies the easygoing, but is not easygoing himself."

★

What would Kate's ad look like?

"Smart, attractive, funny, forgiving, courteous, sympathetic, ambidextrous SWF with weakness for lost causes. Likes marmalade, literature majors, and hiking—but injured her knee playing tennis last year, so trails with a significant elevation gain are out of the question. Can spell anything. Once owned a parakeet named Mikey."

*

Dr. C is convinced his temperament—his comfortableness with himself and others, his cheerfulness—gets in the way of him being thought of as an intellectual.

*

We don't have much in the way of sexual intrigue around here. I suppose the reason is legal. That doesn't mean, of course, there isn't any. For instance, there are some suspicions about Scott and Monica, Patrick Mitchell's secretary. I don't really want to imagine it because Scott is someone I have, on several occasions, almost liked, and Monica—with her malicious prissiness and helmet of red hair—is simply too terrible to contemplate.

*

Peter has stories from the U of O Writing Program that make the hair stand up on the back of my neck. Stories about workshops where pieces are read and commented on by one and all—the qualified and the not. Everyone circles up like scouts around a campfire. They start with a strained observation or two about what they liked, and then get down to the proverbial nitty-gritty—comments about what "hadn't worked," the not-so-subtle hint being that it was something the writer of the piece should consider revisiting, something he or she should fix if they were sensible enough to value their audience.

Peter kept going because he kept hoping there were tricks—things he could learn that would help him find a way to do what he wanted, not simply what he could. There were no tricks. You had to console yourself with making connections—with getting the names of people who knew people who at some point later on could do you favors.

*

Julie Griffin is a perpetual thrower of parties. (I finally stopped getting pro-forma invites after the third decline.) She lives to be dazzling, to glide from room to room pollinating the conversations of this and that clique with a crisp few minutes of inspired chit-chat.

★

It seems like I'm always suspicious of what I feel. I'm afraid I'm trying to fool myself to avoid realizing something that, once realized, could not be ignored.

★

Mary Morganti was a thorn in Peter's side. She was part of a small contingent of conventional convention-flouters who sang-froidly invited him to join their cozy little cabal (their clique of the deeply knowing), who felt they had proffered a rare honor, and who were at first perplexed, then offended, by a typically none-too-tactful Peter-like rebuff—a dismissive, no-frills, thanks-but-no-thanks. She made it her job to plague his paragraphs in almost every read-around.

★

I was mystified at how deeply interested Kate seemed in me. At first I thought it was just that she was deeply interested in everyone, but the more I got to know her the less that seemed to be the case. She is interested in more people than I am, but I can see now that there are limits.

★

There is nothing glamorous about routine, but it does have its virtues. There is the efficiency of it, for instance, and the function of limiting one's exposure to disaster. It's not an easy thing to do when disaster is everywhere.

*

George Fowler tries to have pure thoughts because he believes he is responsible for any and every thing that comes into his head.

*

Nora Simons, Peter's old girlfriend, isn't exactly a stalker, but she isn't exactly not one either. After they broke up she started wandering around nights and weekends looking for him. She went to all the old places, places they had gone together—places he used to live, places they went for dinner, places they shopped for groceries. She would do this to the point of exhaustion, until some stranger had to step up and help her—give her something to eat or to drink or a place to sit down for a minute. Ali Nichols, his new girlfriend, while nonetheless strange, does seem considerably less frightening.

*

Loretta Spikes used to wear the most incredibly terrible perfume—a sort of mint and cantaloupe scent. Lots of it. She was called into HR and asked to cease and desist for environmental reasons. Several people had complained that they were allergic and that it was overpowering to be trapped in the elevator with her.

*

I hate it when Shelly comes into my cubicle to use my fax machine. It's like a weather front of unhappiness and complaint sweeping in. You get the feeling she's had a hard life, grown up in blighted, possibly violent conditions, and that just below the surface of her standard office neighborliness lies a mean and angry person—someone who screams at home and throws things.

*

I was reluctant for a while to have a doctor—it seemed so trivializing. But I've gotten used to it over these last couple of years. While I can't say it exactly feels necessary, it doesn't feel exactly frivolous either— not like Denise's doctor. (She just had to have one—he went with her big house, her ornate manicure, her neurotic chihuahuas.) I've been discussing Dr. C with Kate for quite some time now.

★

When I look back at it I think Mrs. Dorton just hated me on sight. I don't know why. It was in part, I think, one of those inexplicable, spontaneous things—like, for instance, the way I feel about Ted Doss. It didn't help that I once called the police on her.

(She had converted her kitchen into a laboratory where, in her non-apartment-managing hours, she was trying to develop a line of hair-care products for older women. Once or twice a week she stank up the whole building with her experiments. On one especially bad occasion when I was coughing and my eyes were watering and it felt like I had been tear-gassed, I called the police. She got some sort of written warning. She saw me as someone who was slowing things down for her, someone who was getting in the way of her getting rich, someone who was getting in the way of her moving to Florida.)

★

Edward in accounting says he has a girlfriend. He says her name is Amy. I've never met her, never seen a picture of her, never heard him talking to her on the telephone. I have a feeling she is make-believe. I made a joke about this once and he ignored me. He won't discuss her with me at all. He thinks it would be unchivalrous.

★

Poor Dr. C. Because I don't use drugs or drink enough to be classified an alcoholic, he has had to conclude that it's simply the stress of me being me that is playing havoc with my brain chemistry.

*

At one point (I'm not exactly sure how I got there), I was under the impression Mrs. Dorton was not only sneaking into my apartment during the day when I was away, but at night. I noticed strange food smells in the place when I got home, and Toby, normally a gluttonous diner, was not going at his dinner with his usual abandon. I started weighing him before I left and when I got home. There were discrepancies. I started trying to stay awake in the hope of catching her, becoming sleep-deprived and quasi-delirious in the process. I started to get worried about the way things were going when I realized I was wishing, quite seriously, for something terrible to happen to her. It felt that, given the condition I was in, it was only a matter of time before things evolved to the point that I was actively participating in this terrible thing, whatever it was. That is when I went to Dr. Lindsey, the mustachioed glad-hander of days gone by.

*

Peter was telling me about a story he read the other day—an older, quasi-ethnic one recommended to him by someone he almost never pays any attention to. He was struck by the number of breasts that were in it. His dog book doesn't have any breasts in it so far and he is wondering about putting some in. The first sight of Ali's generally lovely pair is indelibly etched in his memory, he said, but he didn't really have any interest in getting all Updikey. Breasts, he says, are an aesthetic mistake in stories such as his.

They are distracting. They have to be handled just right. He says if he does decide to put some in he's going to use my shower story.

(I had read somewhere that it was romantic to take showers by candlelight, so I thought I'd try it. It was, in fact, quite nice for a while. Kate was beautiful—all that slippery nakedness illuminated by soft, warm, flickering yellow light. It was nice until the shower curtain caught on fire. In a moment of panic I tried to stamp it out with my bare foot and got pretty badly burned. Needless to say, it sort of ruined the mood. I had to wear a special shoe for several weeks.)

★

What appears to be indifference may, in fact, be fear.

★

It's about a pointless wandering through an unbounded nothingness.

★

I'm not the sort of person who attracts attention, but Peter is. There is something about him that doesn't seem quite right, and you notice it. I have tried to put my finger on just what that something not quite right is, but I have never succeeded. I think it has something to do with his eyes, with the quality of his gaze—the way he seems to arbitrarily focus on one thing and not another. But then again. . . .

★

Ellery Kovach has a fur hat that is not to be believed. A huge beige thing with flaps—it sits up high on his head. It looks like he's wearing a Koala.

★

I think Dr. C is looking for a breakthrough, something dramatic, a sudden realization on my part that something I thought or felt wasn't really what I thought or felt it to be, but was something else entirely.

I sometimes wish for his sake that I had melodramatic inclinations. The monotonousness of my complaints must make the time go slowly. I can barely stay interested myself. I'd like to entertain him with some flamboyant craziness, but I doubt I could be convincing.

*

John Thayer has twenty-two pairs of sunglasses.

*

Carol Johnson chews her fingernails.

*

Why am I seeing him? This is a question I ask myself with some regularity. I'm not looking for a friend. I'm not looking for a crutch—at least I don't think I am anyway. I guess I am trying to gain a certain perspective in areas where, for one reason or another, I do not trust myself. I'm trying to find ways to use both his expressed and implied suggestions to make it a littler easier being me. I would prefer—if it's possible—that these strategies not involve my becoming someone else, but I know in ruling this out I may be asking the impossible.

THREE

I think that is Darren Kerry out there. He works in payroll. Everyone is nice to the people in payroll because they hope—maybe sometime at lunch—they'll let something slip about how much so-and-so makes or what such-and-such's expense report looked like.

★

Sometimes it isn't the trying that is hard—it's the wanting to try.

★

Susan Taylor's grandfather is ninety-four. He plays the banjo. He gets trotted out by a local television station once or twice a year to amaze us with his derring-do. *Camptown Races* is, of course, a crowd favorite.

★

Bacon, eggs, blueberry pancakes, and coffee.

★

Advice to myself this morning: work with what you have.

*

Kate is one of those people who likes to do something and then remember it over and over again. The whole point of doing it is to have it to remember. Like going to dinner—she will remember over and over what the place looked liked, what the chicken was seasoned with, what I said about the frigid couple seated across from us. Whatever happens is enough for her. There is nothing she can't find something extraordinary about.

*

One problem with it getting hot is not just that it's getting hot, but that everyone has to talk about it getting hot, has to tell you what it feels like out there right now—how many degrees warmer it is this morning at 6:30 than it was yesterday.

*

Peter is talking about another novel for which he has no title but which he thinks he may have just started. He's fighting with himself about it because, while on one hand it is something he wants to write, he can't help thinking he's starting it now as a way of avoiding work on the dog book, which is not turning out to be what he had hoped. He seems discouraged on several levels.

*

Kate's meals are always complicated. She never wants anything the way it is offered. She wants things added and subtracted. She wants things substituted. She wants things prepared in a slightly different fashion. I can't help but wonder what would happen if she saw me on a menu.

*

Being depressed doesn't mean you see life the way it is, but seeing it the way it is (nasty, brutish, and short, for example) just might depress you. There was a time when a faith in God could deliver you—now a pill will. Embrace the fantasy; life is short. Why not fill it with all the pleasure you can? It's an answer. I don't know why I can't accept it.

Dr. C wants to know if I hope to recover. I have to tell him no. If I hope for anything—and I must or I wouldn't be seeing him—it's to find a way of dealing with whatever it is I am dealing with—a way that would leave me with a little more left over.

*

Excerpt from conversation between Jeff Valley and Lee Elton:

"You hear anything about Whitmore?"

"What should I hear?"

"I don't know—about him quitting or getting fired. You hear everything."

"Everyone thinks I hear everything."

"You do."

"I wish I did."

"Who should I ask then?"

"About what?"

"About Whitmore."

"How should I know?"

"Everyone knows you hear everything. If there is anything you haven't heard, you know who has."

"Has what?"

"Who has heard. So?"

"So?"

"So who should I ask about Whitmore, about him quitting or maybe getting fired?"

"Ask Gail. I saw her a little bit ago. She looks pleased with her-self. Ask her."

*

I picked Kate up to go to the movies last night. I got to her place at seven. She wasn't ready. I asked her if she had ever noticed that in all of the time we had been seeing each another, she had never once been ready to go on time. So, she said, let's think of it as one of our traditions.

*

Peter was talking about his dog book in general. He said he didn't know how hard to work on it. Whatever it was going to end up being, it wasn't going to be what he wanted, and he would dis-like it. The more he worked on it the less he would dislike it—but that was only up to a point. The trick was recognizing that point because when he got to it, he would be done.

*

Bonnie Hall likes to be around people who make her look pret-tier—so she likes to be around Judy Cobb, who, being something of a gargoyle, makes everyone look prettier. What she hasn't taken into account is that being around Judy may make you look pret-tier, but it will also make you look stupider because gargoyle or not, Judy is probably the smartest woman in the building. What Bonnie gains in one respect, she loses in another.

*

I think I have to agree. This may be a form of penance.

*

Kate wants to improve the world. Toward that end, she wants to improve me.

*

Linda Moore's father died at a football game. He had a heart attack in overtime. In a way, she says, it was a blessing. His team lost 17-14.

*

When I slip into one of these funks I'm not easily righted. It takes me longer than I think it should to slip out. That can't be good.

*

Excerpt from a conversation between Alex Hartung and Bob Hasenkamp:

"My son is obsessed with frogs."

*

Peter heard from someone who knew someone who knew John Sullivan. John writes book reviews for the local paper. Apparently there is a piece on *Cubicle Dreams* in the works. As always, Peter has mixed emotions. He knows Sullivan's work, likes it, but thinks maybe the guy has gotten tired of having to have opinions about everything. Peter says he has noticed a weariness—it appears in the reviews as an impatience for anything not clear-cut.

*

"They only have so much space. The choices about what does and does not get sacrificed are rarely made in your favor."

*

Frederick Baker doesn't really care for his wife. I wonder what it's like to wake up each morning with someone you're not happy to see.

*

Peter was transformed. From what, I really don't know.

*

Good afternoon Dr. C—another hour of gentlemanly wrestling in the mud?

*

Excerpt from conversation between Randy Usher and Steven Vale:
"She told me last night that she had always wanted to marry a cowboy and that she didn't know what happened because I was about as far away from a cowboy as a person could get."

*

Carolyn Bayless has a sweetness about her that seems too good to be true—an inexplicable, stupefying kind of unconditional approval of almost everything. I find it less depressing to be around the acrimonious types—the knee-jerk disapprovers who, in struggling against whatever it is they're struggling against, at least show some signs of being alive.

*

Ann Olebring was adopted. It's almost the first thing she tells you about herself. I've always wondered why.

*

I wanted to go for Indian food because there is always so much to say about it. A discussion of the exotic tastes and smells can fill almost any awkward silence.

*

Excerpt from conversation between Edward Plumber and Jason Stewart:

"If you don't ignore what you can it's going to be nothing but trouble."

★

As part of a discussion about the virtues of on-demand publishing, Peter brought up a writer of experimental fiction famous in certain egghead circles for being unknown and underappreciated. Peter has read several of his books. Artfully arranged conglomerations of cultural curiosities—getting into one was like getting into a bag of potato chips: once you started, you couldn't stop. Peter saw an interview in which this writer discussed the difficulty he had finding a publisher for one of the most admired of his admired-but-unknown books. He thought he had set some sort of record for rejections. Donleavy had gotten 36 for *The Ginger Man*, Beckett had gotten 42 for *Murphy*—he had gotten 54. Peter was appalled by the waste of time, energy, hope, and postage. With this new technology—with digital printing and on-demand publishing—a marginal writer just didn't have to go through that now.

★

For Heather Nance, there isn't anything better than going to a party. For me, there are few things worse—maybe going to a shopping mall or a grade school.

★

Peter's author photo isn't especially good, but you have to like that long, sad, serious face. If nothing else, it says this is someone you should give a chance to.

★

Priscilla Hahn wants us to believe that she believes she talks to her dead sister. She thinks it makes her more interesting—in fact, it makes her less.

⋆

Peter has a number of ideas, but he gave up trying to organize them a long time ago.

⋆

I've always thought it would be nice to be certain about something.

⋆

Peter is excited. He just heard that Anna King, kind-hearted Renaissance woman and proprietress of Wonderland Books, had agreed to stock *Cubicle Dreams*.

⋆

I would rather the relationship was with you; and you, understandably enough, seem to prefer it was with your prescription pad. Prescribing certainly seems the manlier thing to do—I mean, it's clearly more virile than a lot of nervous nattering.

⋆

Yes, but can we trust what I say about myself? At what point should I assume you are a better judge than I am of what I'm thinking?

⋆

Peter and Ali were already there when we arrived. They had been seated and were studying the menu. The evening hasn't begun and already I'm behind.

*

Douglas Faro is an amateur magician. He is always pulling silk scarves out of his clenched fist and making ping-pong balls disappear.

*

I made the introductions as graciously as I could. Everyone shook everyone else's hand. For some reason Ali wanted to know if Kate spelled her name with a "C" or a "K."

*

From the way Brian Huggett walks down the hall, you get the feeling he knows where he is going.

*

Marie Inger has a three-year-old son. He is always ill.

*

By way of conversation, Peter thought it would be interesting if Kate would discuss Dr. Hinkle's personal life. She declined. Peter, of course, persisted. Kate said she was sorry but it wasn't really a subject she felt comfortable with.

I tried to muddy the waters a little with a long non sequitur—a story about a time I went skin-diving and was stung by a jellyfish.

*

Gary Montgomery is a woodworker.

*

Kate takes her sweet time with a menu. She always has questions for the waitress—three at least.

★

Angie Hobbs is afraid of the radiation from mobile phones. She won't stand next to anybody who is using one.

★

John Libby has been mugged twice in Old Town.

★

Kate choked on a piece of tandoori. It was terrible. Her face turned red; she couldn't catch her breath. I pounded her on the back harder and harder. Eventually that did it. She could breathe again. Her eyes were watering, but, other than that, all of her systems seemed to return to business as usual. It's sickening to feel so helpless. There is nobody less prepared for a medical emergency than I am.

★

Excerpt from conversation between Ed Lee and Alan Hall:
"Have you ever tried warm milk? As an adult, I mean. It's terrible—and it doesn't work."

★

Ali has a wonderful effect on Peter. Something about her relative normalcy seems to settle him.

★

The real trouble begins when you can't, in your own mind, turn your suffering into something heroic—when it is simply suffering and not the price you have to pay for some plucky act of witness.

★

Kate sees how I am with Peter, which isn't just different in the subtle ways you would expect from the ways I am with her, but in some other, more sinister way—a way that makes her nervous. She has not allowed herself to formulate any long-term plans, but the ones that are floating out there unformulated, whatever they are, are in jeopardy because of something she senses about this side of me, the side she sees when I'm with him. She didn't know it, of course, but a fear that this would be the case is really what was behind her reluctance to meet Peter in the first place. It wasn't actually him who she didn't want to meet—it was me with him. She suspected to some extent that I would be the way I apparently am and that if I was that way and she saw it, she would have to be worried about our future together—and if she had to be worried about our future, our present could be compromised.

*

Any time he does something reprehensible he flatters himself by thinking of it as an attack on the middle class.

*

Martha Flynn is a tall, skinny, vegetarian who confines her diet not just to vegetables, but to certain vegetables grown in a certain way. She thinks exactly what you would expect her to think about the political situation at home and abroad. I find her annoying—in part, because she doesn't like me. I don't mind being disliked, as I think I've said before, but that's if I'm disliked for a reason. Martha doesn't have a reason. She barely knows me. She dislikes me because she dislikes me. The correctness of her beliefs (and the attending glow of sanctimony) together with her disliking me for no reason combine to make her unique for me. I feel about a lot of people the way I feel about Nathan, but I don't think I feel about anyone else the way I do about Martha.

*

Peter is, among other things, reclusive. All of the stuff that goes on now around writing—conferences, retreats, workshops, publishing parties, interviews, book tours—give him the willies. Yet one more reason to publish his work himself.

*

Craig Sanders is a germaphobe. He is at the sink washing his hands with a frightening vigor when Martin Davis sticks his head in the door. Martin wants to know if anyone has seen me.

So it begins. The rumors I've been trying to ignore are probably not rumors. Things are afoot. Happenings are happening. Some sort of reorganization is underway, and for reasons known only to the powers that be, Mitchell wants to put me on Nathan Locke's team. I don't want to be on Nathan Locke's team. I don't like Nathan Locke. I don't like him in a fundamental and serious way. He is one of those people who has something to prove, which means he's a menace to those of us who don't. He's married to Debra Fuller, bitchy blonde daughter of Walter Fuller, one of the VPs on the money-making side of this place.

*

Thank you Dr. C for the sneaky dissertation on cortical function and its relation to world view. I'll never look at rational positivism the same again.

*

The job that is going to be offered isn't the sort of job that really matters—the sort you might enjoy, the sort it is possible to be proud of. That sort of job exists here, but not in this department. The job I'm going to be offered is just a larger, more conspicuous version of the job I have now. I don't want it. When the time comes that I have to make that fact known to the muckety-mucks in charge, I'll be setting processes in motion—processes that will ultimately lead to my having to leave I think.

★

Beware of your automatic thoughts.

★

Rollin Teller is very proud of his ability to open beer bottles with his teeth.

★

I have a feeling that what lies at the heart of my uneasiness with Dr. C is his inclination to see philosophical issues as psychiatric ones and psychiatric ones as medical—*i.e.*, chemical. Too much this, not enough that—get the formula right and the metaphysics will follow.

★

Arithmetic is pretty but pitiless.

★

For me, this is probably the best place the company has to offer. The next-best place might be endurable, but not for long.

FOUR

I am not a person with a lot of friendliness in him. I don't feel nearly as bad about this as I'm supposed to—something I'm sure at some point Dr. C will want to get into.

Most of the friendliness I do have in me is spent here at work so there is not a whole lot left over for the neighbors. I try to know them as little as I can. There is Arthur Spinnett. He is divorced and pitiful and works in the computer industry. Just the sight of him puts me in a bad mood.

Then there are the Hartmans, Raymond and Maureen, in 805. They're from Australia. They have accents, and they're always letting their half-tailed cat, Frenzy, run loose in the halls. I see Maureen often. She is one of those people who have a tendency to lurk. I dread our little encounters because we don't really have anything to say to each another—a fact that hasn't stopped us from feeling we have to try. This invariably means an exchange of banalities about the weather—it's either too cold, too hot, too cloudy, too dry, too wet, or beautiful. We discuss it as if it were news, as if our opinions about it were unusually informed and our thoughts perspective-producing and profound. Is this amount of rain too much or is it the amount a reasonable person should expect given the longitude, latitude, and time of year. My preference is for dark and cold, but I keep this to myself because I'm not really interested in Maureen knowing my preferences about anything, let alone the weather. I have no interest in convincing her that, as preferences about the weather go, they are superior to hers (warm and bright, no doubt)—although I think there is a tricky big-picture argument to be made to this effect. I never object to her initial characterization of the day until we start hitting 80 degrees. At that point I can no longer give her a neighborly nod of validation. 80 degrees is too hot. I feel compelled to say so out of respect for the truth.

⋆

Leo Gerdes has the hairiest forearms in the department. It's scary to imagine what his back must look like.

⋆

The first thing you think about Lisa when you meet her is that this is someone who cares too much about being thin. It's important to her. It's always on her mind. She makes innumerable calculations and adjustments to her day in service to the idea. But it's a certain sort of thin, a decorative sort—not the sort that starts you speculating about neurotic eating disorders.

She thinks that because I'm inaccessible to her I'm inaccessible to Kate and that that inaccessibility will have catastrophic consequences in the long run. She thinks if Kate were to commit herself to me in the conventional sense, she would end up being one of those lonely women who start drinking early in the day, who flirt pathetically at parties, who wear too much makeup—that is, she is afraid Kate would become a woman very much like her mother. Understandably, she doesn't want that for her friend.

*

Delaney!

*

Sometimes it seems the things I believe are so diffuse. It's not that I really want them to cohere, to bunch up into a unified, arguable philosophy of life, but it would be nice to have some lumps here and there in one's theoretical oatmeal. It would make sorting things out so much easier.

*

Peter's father died when he was nine. I'm not really inclined to make as much of this as some. I'm going to mention it and move on. It's a fact that seems to say less and less about him with each passing year.

*

I don't know what Kate said to Lisa about the other evening, but apparently it was emboldening. She has started to press Kate again about playing the field, about looking around a little before she gets too heavily involved.

*

Having a heat wave. We're supposed to set a record for the date today. That's one of those possibilities that just sort of squats on my day. I can't get it out of my mind. I hate the heat. I can't think about anything else. I can't feel anything else. I had a chocolate chip cookie at lunch. It made me sick. I won't be able to have another one for I don't know how long. Who can tolerate a temperature that does that to you—puts you off chocolate chip cookies.

*

Tammy Kean is one of those people who seems to think that if she were friendly enough—if she brought you banana bread from home or her old copies of *People* magazine—you might, from time to time, make mistakes in her favor.

*

I am a worrier. I'm never in the moment. I'm always looking ahead for trouble, for things going wrong, for things getting in some way worse, for disaster. I can never relax.

*

In Peter's novel I am turned into a monster by a lack of sleep. I come up with a plan to rid myself of my tormenter, Mrs. Dorton. I rent a car and lay in wait for her to make her nightly pilgrimage to the Kingston where she has a beer or two with her friend, Deanna Redell. When she turns down the alley behind the Jim Fisher Volvo Dealership, I will run her over—not a lot, but a little: just enough to put her in the hospital so I can have a few nights of undisturbed sleep, clear my head, make adjustments and plans for the future. Perhaps there will be a miscalculation, an overcorrection, and she will be killed? Peter hasn't decided.

*

Jim Hatch owes a large part of his success here to the quality of his golf game.

*

Norma Conklin wears glasses, has stringy hair, and is unable to make eye contact. If she doesn't play the oboe, she should.

*

Dr. C made some sort of passing comment about my bookwormishness. He wanted to know if I could elaborate a little. I said I could, but I was reluctant as it was an immensely complex subject and I wasn't prepared in the way I would like to be to hold forth meaningfully on it.

But . . . ?

But, in short—literature being in essence a concentrated form of exceptional experience—reading was to me a way of filling one's life with as much of the best as one could.

⋆

Excerpt from a conversation between William Brinker and Timothy Brooks, our resident movie buffs (they are having a debate about who is funnier—Groucho Marx or W. C. Fields. Bill says Groucho. Tim says W.C. It's like a tennis match. Bill serves a Groucho line, Tim returns with a Fields.):

"Who are you going to believe, me or your own eyes?"

"A thing worth having is a thing worth cheating for."

"I never forget a face, but in your case I'll be glad to make an exception."

"Some weasel took the cork out of my lunch."

"I've had a perfectly wonderful evening. But this wasn't it."

"Cross my heart and hope to eat my weight in goslings."

"I don't have a photograph, but you can have my footprints. They're upstairs in my socks."

⋆

Lisa's position is that Kate thinks about me too much, and that's not good. It means there are too many things about me that need considering and that she is giving up time she should be spending on other stuff—herself, for example—to focus on me.

★

What is the worst that can happen? I can almost never answer that. The answers I do manage are feeble and fail to convey fully the nature and breadth of the disaster I imagine.

★

Dr. C is worried about the weakness of my affiliative drive—as were my previous doctors. (As am I myself.) I don't know how many times he has brought up the subject of support. I think he has a point and that, in fact, he is right—we're social animals. It's just not something I can see really working for me. If things were turned around and I was the one being asked to provide encouragement, what would I say to someone like me that could possibly make a difference? Nothing, that's what. Some burdens simply must be borne. They are not amenable to being lightened or off-loaded.

★

Marilynn is a rarity in my experience—a woman who whistles. She is one of my favorite people here. I like her a lot. Tall, round, with watery eyes and a runny red potato nose, she is probably the funniest person in the building. She used to live in New York. She was a wild woman. Something happened. I don't know what, but I get the feeling she has been hiding out ever since.

★

I am worried that Kate will get bored with me because I am, for the most part, boring. Because she is inherently kind, she will not be able to admit this—that I am boring. She will see it as her inability to comprehend the scintillating essence of the extravaganza that is me. She will blame herself.

*

Jeanette Robins has white hair that she piles in a roll on top of her head. It looks like she is wearing a turban made of cotton candy. I'm a little suspicious of her. I have a feeling she is someone who wants to be fascinating.

*

It seems like I'm always filled with a low-level dread, a fear that something bad is going to happen, something that will require my time and attention—things I don't have to spare, things that I've committed to the maintenance of a certain sort of equilibrium.

I haven't wondered why I am this way as much as I should. I have, in fact, avoided wondering about it because even though I believe in the truth in a way that I don't believe in much of anything else, I have never thought of it as setting you free. I have, in fact, imagined it as being imprisoning as frequently as not.

Why am I the way I am and not some other, better way? Neither of my parents have died unexpectedly nor been caught by me at an early age *in flagrante delicto*. My older sister did not dress me in doll clothes nor has a beloved and trusted brother poked my eye out with a flaming stick. If I have been traumatized, it has been by myself, by coming nose-to-nose in the dark with a snarling, bad-smelling, organ-liquefying sense of insignificance.

*

Waiting for this job offer is exhausting. The job I have is small and boring, but Shafer's job isn't the answer. Nothing that is going to be offered is going to be better. It's going to be worse. I'd like something a little less dreary, a little less small—but not a lot. I need to have enough left at the end of the day, enough to put into the projects that sustain me. The balance is a delicate one—a little less dreary, a little less small. I don't think it's the sort of job that exists anywhere. It certainly doesn't exist here.

★

I've asked Peter to change Toby's name, but he won't. He says he would if he could, but he can't because Toby is the perfect name for this character—anything else would be second-best, a blight on the project.

★

Dr. C, please consider this: you can—without trying—be in two places at one time.

★

Right now Jeff Spear's daughter wears braces and is flat-chested, but the day will come when the braces go and the bra appears and he will have to become what he fears becoming most—a father, the person who stands between you and everything you want in life.

★

Sometimes it feels like a game. It doesn't tell us anything about anything, but it makes it easier to get up in the morning if we pretend it does.

★

Told Dr. C that I couldn't see him the other day as I had gotten myself into a little scheduling jam. It wasn't true. I just needed a break. Sometimes I just get tired of him—tired of his proselytizing for a peppier view of things, tired of his relentless efforts to appear reasonable yet caring. Sometimes the prospect of fifty fun-filled minutes of his leading me inexorably toward the light is just too daunting.

★

I don't think of myself as a pessimist, but obviously I am one. For example, the first time I saw Kate I started thinking about the last time I would see her. I imagined some sort of relationship almost immediately, and, judging from past experience, one that would fail. (See Annette, Pam, Linda, Laurie, and Rebecca.) It would have to be some time in the summer—nothing good ever happens in the summer. We are at the apartment. She is moving out. She is waiting for me to say something that would make things right, but I can't because I have no idea what the right thing to say might be. We will try to be exemplary about it—civil beyond civil because whatever else is going on, civility is something we both admire unreservedly. We will talk about how strange it is that somehow something that started so wonderfully could have come to this, but that it has—and now that it has, we have no choice but to honor the reality of it. We don't know why we are doing this really—only that for some reason it now seems compulsory, it now seems it has to be done.

★

This is the second time this year we have traced our colds back to Patricia Watkins. She won't stay home when she is sick. She thinks she is being strong. We think she is being inconsiderate.

★

Richard Lee has a twin brother.

★

It's hard sitting here with this memo pad and no hope. Waiting for what—the beginning of all sorts of unhappiness. He'll make the offer, I'll decline. I'll be forced to quit. I'll go out on interviews but I won't be able to find a job because I won't be able to fake the necessary enthusiasm for the various positions. Everything will go to zero—my bank balance, the number of items in my refrigerator, the number of days left before the electricity is turned off. I'll take a job as a part-time bartender. I'll work with a bearded guy named Dennis, a guy in his fifties who looks like a wine-barrel with legs. He will lecture me about being able to anticipate people's needs. It will last about two days. In desperation I'll take a job delivering pizza from which I'll be kidnapped and killed by a pair of tattooed cretins robbing me for drug money.

★

When I first heard about this other guy I remember wondering what he looked like—which, of course, made me wonder about what I looked like. I was a little surprised at how rarely I had thought about this. I guess if you boil everything down, the most you can say for me is that I'm average-looking and not fat. This means, of course, that as a physical specimen, I'm hoping he is nothing special.

★

Susan Griggs wishes she had a secret, something glamorously tragic that would explain some of her unexplainable behavior, something she could go on television and admit to a national audience, something she could cry about, something the host of the show would praise her for having had the photogenic courage to reveal. But she doesn't have a secret. All she has is world enough and time. Time to disappoint. Time to worry. Time to come and go. Time to talk of Fra Angelico.

★

At some point the question seems to have changed. It's no longer "who am I?" but "what should I wear?"

*

Dennis Chamberlin's daughter is going to Princeton in the fall. He thinks this reflects well on him so he finds a way to mention it about once a week. We will all be glad when she gets there and flunks out.

*

Kate's friend and I don't seem to be able to glance at one another without exchanging looks. Hers to me seems one of pure reproach. I don't have any idea what mine to her is supposed to be—puzzled dislike, I guess.

*

Debbie Fletcher has been talking about her new-found passion for bicycling. My impersonation of an interested third-party was, I think, impeccable.

*

I saw two nuns at lunch. It was very strange. I never really thought of them as having to eat. It didn't look right—ancient, wrinkled women dressed in elaborate habits, each with her own fat hamburger.

*

There is nothing comfortable-seeming about Dr. C's office. The furniture looks new and unused—a bit like Dr. C himself. The desk and chairs are generic examples—but expensive. It's always a little cold, which I like, and a little brightly lit, which I don't. We sit across from each other in a sort of nook, a small walnut coffee table between us. There are Ansel Adam prints everywhere.

*

Excerpt from conversation between Leonard Dunbar and Paul Gonzales:

"She wants to know if I think she looks funny. She overheard someone saying something at work, and she thinks they might have been talking about her."

*

Lisa believes she has an exceptional sixth sense. She hardly has to think about a thing at all—she just knows. For instance, she just knows I'm not the right guy for Kate.

*

Peter knows how I feel about Toby, but he said for my own good he was going to make me promise never to write an essay about him. The chances of it turning out to be anything but maudlin are almost nil.

*

Dr. C is convinced I'm depressed—in part, because I don't seem to think more of myself. I've tried to explain that I was just responding to his questions, that my feelings in this area are not something I found burdensome. I do not think of myself as worthless, but neither do I see myself as someone of particularly high value. Yes, I have a tendency to be despondent, and, yes, I occasionally worry that at some point these feelings will become unmanageable. I don't think it means I'm depressed—not clinically anyway, as he has implied. It just means I'm a realist and not very much fun.

*

Everyone keeps asking me if Janet (a female character who appears in several of Peter's stories) is really Ali (Peter's real-life inamorata). They also keep asking Ali if she is Janet. When I answer, I say yes, sometimes one is the other, but that I'd guess about 95% of the time they aren't.

★

Maggie Watt's mother is the only person I know who owns a mink coat.

★

Lisa has problems and so is predisposed to be impatient with people similarly afflicted. There is her weight for one thing—a constant struggle if we are to believe her complaints. There is also simple decency. It doesn't come naturally to her the way it does to Kate—she has to work at it.

★

Everyone has been whispering about Angela Waters. The rumor is she was fired from her previous job under suspicious circumstances. We think she might be a thief.

★

When I think of Gary Zimmerman, I think of profanity. People in his line of work just don't swear like that anymore.

★

Lisa's relationship with Bart has been going through a calm patch lately so getting involved in Kate's relationship with me gives her something to do. Sometimes she likes to call a friend of hers, Kelly, and have everyone meet for lunch—where they will, of course, compare notes on the men in their lives. Kate swears she doesn't really say that much about me at these get-togethers, but I can't believe what she does say does me any good. I can't

measure up very well against Kelly's Dennis, the bearded veteri-
narian with a heart of gold, or Lisa's significant other, Bart, the
friendly musician with a day job (insurance sales). The only thing
that can distract them from an analysis of my shortcomings is
one of Kelly's diatribes. She is very happy with Dennis, but after a
glass of wine she invariably has something to say about his father,
Arthur.

*

Another dicey session with Dr. C. I told him that, contrary to
his not-so-veiled suggestion, I did on some level understand that
there were people in this world whose lives were not periodically
circumscribed by anxiety and dread. I said that while I envied
them, I did not trust or revere them.

*

The only thing we know about Alan Thomas is that he is per-
petually rumpled and lives alone. I would love to get a look inside
his apartment. I'm sure it's filled with clues.

*

Yes, doc, let's wander around my childhood—see if we can
spot something to hang a diagnosis on.

*

At heart, one thing Peter and I share is a belief that ideas can
and do enrich your everyday life.

*

Have you noticed this coffee never cools off? You can sit around
sipping it all morning, but you can never actually drink it.

*

Kathy Clementi likes being a mistress. She thrives on the drama.

★

Sometimes, Dr. C, I'm surprised. I never knew it was possible to feel this bad for no good reason.

★

Does Charlene Iverson know what she looks like in that outfit? Is it really what she intended?

★

Me and my delicateness. It sure can get tiring. Oh woe is me… I'm in the deep dark dumps. How long can you listen to that? You would have to pay me too—I mean, how many times can you ask a person if they're all right before you stop really caring about the answer?

★

We pretend I am brave because I am here, but I can't believe in our heart of hearts that either of us feels this is true. I think really I'm just looking for a way to abdicate responsibility, a way to flatter myself. I'm a victim of circumstance—the sum of my syndromes. It would be nice to feel about things the way Tom, Dick, and Harry do—but it isn't going to happen, not without a prescription. You think I need to accept myself. I don't. I think I need to be improved. Wouldn't it be wonderful if somehow we were both wrong?

★

Excerpt from conversation between Dale Cooley and Daniel Hauck:

"If I had it to do over again I think I'd be a gastroenterologist or a ski bum."

★

I know you've been doing this for a while, that when you look at me you start checking things off mentally—my appearance in relation to my age, am I guarded, agitated, cooperative? What about my rate of speech, my fluency? Am I sad, happy, flat? How many presidents can I name? You'll make some notes. You'll have a sense that whatever it is that is bothering me is something that can be named and, in the end, one way or another, managed. I don't really need you to believe that, but I find it comforting that you do.

★

Mark Allen likes to get calls from the office when he's on vacation. It makes him feel large and indispensable.

★

Yes, Dr. C, my beady-eyed bird-watcher, where do I fall on the continuum—what twitches and disorders add up to me? Which parts just are and which can be expected to come and go?

★

I know a lot of time and money has gone into the development and production of this pill, but that does not predispose me to embrace it as the thinking man's answer to the second coming.

★

I know in some ways it would be a great help to you if I were to start taking this. If I did and there was no discernable improvement, there would be a world of things we could rule out. Well, let's leave them in. Let's find another way of naming this whim of mine, another way of filling in that blank space on my form.

★

There is something about Jeffrey Parker's voice—his tone. No matter what he is saying it always sounds like he is trying to sell you something.

★

I know sometimes you need to feel more like you are doing something (and I would like to feel more like something is being done)—but for the sake of something larger I think we should resist these inclinations.

★

There are weeks when Peter will wear the same clothes over and over.

FIVE

Kathleen Bridges has a parrot with a six-hundred-word vocabulary.

★

Frank Hayes is one of those guys who is afraid his son—slim, pale, fearful of insects—is going to grow up to be a homosexual. He thinks if he is resolute in his effort not to notice certain things, they will somehow miraculously cease to be.

★

I get the feeling Patrick Mitchell would like to lose his temper more often—say crueler things more loudly—but has trained himself not to. He has probably noticed in the past that certain people have had a tendency to stay upset when he did this. It took everyone too long to get back on good terms. His lack of polish would hurt him if he had any further ambitions here.

★

It would have been nice if Kate had been sitting at the table this morning saying something outrageous. Something I could pass on around here, something about X, Y, or Z, something brutally honest and cynical, something that cut through the bullshitty niceness of most first-thing-in-the-morning sentiments. But she was not. It was just me and my bowl of granola.

*

When I decline the job I will be letting him down.

*

Sometimes, Dr. C, you get that worried look. I know you try to hide it, but you guys are not the only ones who have learned how to be hyper-vigilant. Some of us crazies have too. Don't worry, I'm not really just one misunderstanding away from a meltdown. If I had to guess, I'd say it was more like five or six.

*

Jim Davis has a precocious daughter with a contrived name that alludes to some sort of astrological phenomenon. Nothing is ever good enough for her. She complains about the various electronic devices they have given her and the furniture in her bedroom. Apparently none of these things meet minimal standards. They reflect poorly on her as a person of evolved contemporary taste and on them as providers.

*

I hate airports. I'm almost phobic about them. They are horrible places. Walk in and you can feel it in the chilled air—the fear, the anxiety. There are some pockets of excitement—of loved ones returning—but mostly it is a heartless dome of worry. Worry about getting your ticket, about getting your boarding pass, about getting through security—worry about missing flights, about getting a seat, about lost luggage, about missing a connection, about losing your mind in Denver, about dying in a fiery crash. The places stink of overpriced concessions and wasted time.

★

Wayne Rutledge is the department hypochondriac. He is always imagining he has a tumor.

★

Like my having time away from Mrs. Dorton changed my perspective, I'm afraid Kate having time away from me will change hers. I have no idea what her new perspective might be, but I can't imagine it would be better than her old perspective.

★

Gordon Shively's suits are just a little too expensive.

★

Peter gave me a scene from a new story he was working on: a father and daughter are walking in the park, behind them a placid pond complete with ducks. The father is recently divorced from the girl's mother. It is one of those awkward weekend outings where they are, in the beginning anyway, trying to keep in touch. The daughter, who is fifteen, is sloppily dressed and sad-faced. She is determined to be miserable. The divorce is new and she wants to luxuriate in the tragic horribleness of it. The father, temperamentally an optimist, doesn't want to indulge her in this because it is anathema to him, and, knowing his daughter's tendency to be overly dramatic, he is reluctant to believe fully in the genuineness of her sorrow. He suspects it is less the way she actually feels than the way she would like to actually feel—her life up to this point having been so privileged and pleasant as to be virtually bereft of crisis. She wants desperately to be the victim of something fun to suffer, something she can share with her friends, something she can recover from—but not too quickly. She wants to be seen as being brave by someone to whom seeming brave is important. He tries to explain that he is not sad, lonesome, or devastated, but she is having none of it. It's just him doing what he always does.

*

He may not have said anything at all, but still he drones. It's a matter of demeanor.

*

I don't think that, as a rule, I look like the sort of person you can talk to—which is just as well because I'm not.

*

Excerpt from conversation between Pat Short and Kevin Spinelli:

"It's a good economical car. I've got no problem with it."

*

I think you are trying to be especially responsive today. Is it possible you have taken some sort of vow? Are you trying to see me as something more than a type?

*

I try to prepare in some way for the misfortunes that I think are coming in the hope of minimizing their consequences. This does not mean I'm prepared. There is a school of thought that suggests there is some comfort to be had in knowing you have done all you can. Not for me. For me, when it arrives—whatever it is—that's what matters. It doesn't mean anything to me that I have done my best if my best is not good enough.

★

Darren Taylor is one of those guys caught in the middle between his mother and his wife. So far they have fought one another to a draw, but before long the wife will tire of this, realize how grievously she has been injured by his emotional equivocation, and retreat—first into bitter sarcasm, then into affairs. I am guessing the divorce is about five years away.

★

You wouldn't know it to look at him, but Kevin Horn was once handcuffed by the police.

★

Janet Valle is always wanting to introduce me to someone. We'll be talking in the hallway about something, and a word will set her off—oh, you know, I should introduce you to Jennifer Walls, to Kristina White, to Lynn Cooper. Why? Apparently she wants everyone she knows to know everyone else she knows. I'm guessing—as I never seem to know anyone she does—that I strike her as especially bereft of acquaintances.

★

In one of Peter's stories I remember meeting a character whose brother had been institutionalized. This brother is sitting in his room doodling on a large pad of paper. He was making a list. He titled the page: "Things I Would Buy If I Were Better." It included:

solid oak dresser
one-day guided rafting trip (lunch included)
special edition bagless upright vacuum cleaner
white 1998 Honda Civic with air conditioning

*

Bob Forsythe is always explaining the latest thinking out of Washington to me. This morning it was all about some ambassadorial nomination and the deviousness of Democrats. Bob is a clever guy, but it's easy to discount his opinions—if for no other reason than his mustache.

*

Excerpt from a conversation between Charles Lewis and Daniel West:

"You know, you can listen to someone talking about their diet for only so long. At some point you're going to start hoping they choke to death on one of those rice cakes."

*

I have said something that has in some way hurt her feelings. I didn't intend to, but that will be considered somehow beside the point. She will want me to say something, but she won't let on what it is. She will just wait for me to pick it out of the air like some sort of radio transmission—and if I don't...well, this is evidence against me.

*

Carol Phillips just had a birthday. All she'll say about it is that it was significant and that it had a zero in it. Well, she isn't thirty, and she probably isn't fifty, so. . . . Big mystery.

*

I have to ration my high spirits. I don't want them to run out before the end of the week.

★

These two love to talk about the newest, most expensive restaurants—clean, elegant, shiny-surfaced places that suggest at first sight the flawless sophistication of a class so different from my own as to be that of another species. The fewer things one can glean from a freshly printed menu, the better. The trick, of course, is to appear sublimely comfortable here—comfortable not from some sort of philosophical indifference to the tonier elements of the ambience, but from belonging, from fitting in, from being a well-scrubbed, folded, razor-sharp, money-making contribution to the spirit of the place.

★

I recall a time in the distant past when I was adaptable. I did things on the spur of the moment. I went places I had never been before with people I did not know. My carelessness seems like a miracle to me.

★

The close attention you have to pay. . . . Don't you ever wish you were in some other line of work—something trival that didn't just wear you down to nothing every day?

★

Gina is immaculate. She is one of three immaculates in the building—women who are so meticulously groomed as to appear flawless. They look like they have been kept wrapped in tissue. It is incredible the time and care they put into this hyper-hygienic illusion.

*

Quit—then what? Move? It's hard. For some (me) almost impossible, but I understand that once you get started it's not so bad. You reassess your life. I remember some straight-shooter telling me that you get into a rhythm of throwing things away. Move. Start over. Pretend you're a better person—one who sympathizes and sleeps well at night.

*

Angela Nichols and Celia Rippe were walking through the lobby on the way to lunch laughing about the travails of toilet training. It gave me the shivers. To be double-crossed at such an early age—by your mother no less.

*

Lisa is afraid that because of me Kate will stop being the way she is. She's afraid the stress of living with me and my disorders will cause Kate to deteriorate, turn into someone sad, someone painful to contemplate. She tells her we have already had the best times we are going to have together and that from now on things will only get worse. Kate doesn't listen now, but I can't help but feel there is going to come a time when she will.

*

Conversation between Sean Edwards and Tom Rivers:
"Geography. Why geography? You interested in that sort of stuff?"
"No, not really. It was just the fastest way out—the fastest way to graduate. They had the fewest requirements."

*

Lisa thinks things are bad for Kate—worse than Kate is letting on. She thinks Kate is trying to protect her from the horrible truth for her sake because she has had her own terrible time with someone like me, and she knows Kate would not want her to get started thinking about all that again.

★

Sometimes I'm inclined to give Peter credit for not going completely nuts or jumping in front of a bus. A humble achievement, but his own.

★

Brad Sayles is one of those people who get loud when they get drunk. I've noticed that, as a rule, these are never the sort of people I seem to want to know.

★

I was in the store last night buying ice cream (mint chocolate chip, if you must know) when I saw Bob Park, the guy who cuts my hair. He didn't see me, and I didn't want him to. It would have been just too strange, too depressingly awkward. I slipped out into the parking lot and waited until I saw him leave before I went back in. I thought about how much stranger it would have been to have seen you. I would have done the same thing, but with greater urgency. I wouldn't have wanted anything to do with an encounter like that. I wouldn't want to see you as an ordinary person in any way if I didn't have to. I mean, I know you are, but I suspend that knowledge as best I can in favor of the half-formed idea that you are something more because if you are, it would seem more likely that you would be able to help. I wouldn't want to see what you had in your shopping basket—it would cause me to lose some vital respect for you. I do not want to know that you buy frozen dinners—things like meatloaf or macaroni and cheese. It would completely alter my view of you—and not for the better. Nobody's shopping does them proud. And what about you noticing something I had in my basket? You have to admit, there would probably be something there that would make you feel differently about me, maybe something that would make you suspicious about something I've said to you in session.

I know you try to be very careful about the way I see you— that you are aware that I look on what you do for a living with a sort of fascinated horror. Or I assume you're aware of this as it hasn't been exactly hidden in the things I've said to you on or around the subject. There are rules, aren't there, about the way you are supposed to act if you run into a patient in the real world? I mean, aren't you suppose to ignore me as much as possible— that is, as much as you can and still come off as empathetic and human. I mean, you'd have to acknowledge me, wouldn't you, if for no other reason than to avoid making the lack of acknowledgment an issue that would take up however much of our next session's agenda.

Would you find my complaints about your coldness hurtful? Would you think I was saying these things to make myself feel better? Will you seize on my fear of injury as an explanation of what you call my "isolation"? Will you want to know if there are specific things about you that bother me? Will you berate me (gently) for not listing them? Can we just label me "avoidant" and call it a day? Can you hear me clearly or does some little closet flaw prevent you from recognizing what you should?

★

Incomplete. Relative. Uncertain.

*

Doug Holmes is old enough now to think that he is wise so we are always having to listen to him proclaim on the big picture: forgive yourself, assume anybody can do anything, you can be a loser no matter how many times you win. It's basically pretty harmless stuff, but over the course of time it can get a little wearing.

*

Conversation between James Law and Jordon Monk:

"She's always reading some damn book and making me take a test about relationships. I never pass any of them."

*

Please, Dr. C, don't give me that look. You know the one I mean—the innocent-bystander one, the victim-of-some-need-of-mine one. It's beneath you. You're subtler than that.

*

Peter is suspicious of those who allow consciousness of their audience to slip into their work. He thinks it compromises the thing. Of course, this is not always bad. Often enough what is compromised is not something that really warranted being kept sacrosanct.

*

Every time we kiss I end up wearing her lipstick. I complain. She tells me she has chosen this particular shade because it looks good on me.

*

I haven't decided whether I can or cannot tolerate boredom. I don't know if my reaction to it is typical or extreme. It's not impossible for me to believe that I put an awful lot into putting up with it, which might explain the depth of my fatigue.

*

I have a feeling that Lisa is not really happy unless there is something wrong between her and Bart. In large part it seems the point of having a boyfriend is to have someone you and your girlfriends can complain about.

*

From our discussion of the shower scene Peter moved on to talk about his dog book in general. He said he was not going to put much sex in it. There were the aesthetic reasons (already mentioned), but also he thought the readers who were after that sort of thing could easily go elsewhere. If there was one thing there was no shortage of in this day and age, it was graphic description. He had nothing against it in its place, but in a certain sort of work he felt it was rarely anything but a mistake. He was willing to concede it was something that could be done well and that it had been done well, but he doubted it was a talent of his so he was moving on with little regret.

*

Diana Peters is someone you have to be careful with—one wrong word and she'll be telling you her whole life story.

*

I keep expecting Kate to be embarrassed by me. She would probably be upset if she was—especially if she was and I noticed. But so far, she hasn't been. What, if anything, does this mean?

*

I had a dream last night that I had hanged myself.

*

Dr. C, it's not that I'm thinking of leaving you—I'm not. It's just that I wondered what you did—how you handled it—when a patient stopped coming. Did you feel abandoned? Did you see it as a criticism of your character or your considerable skill? Did you think they sensed in you a weakness for theory?

*

I know you want to feel a certain way about me and that you worry you might not be able to because I am the sort of person I am.

*

Ran into Maureen on the elevator. She was coming back from the store. Her shopping bag was full of cat food and lottery tickets.

*

Why don't I remember the name of anyone I meet? I always have to meet them again for it to stick—and even then it's not a sure thing.

*

Prove it.

*

Margie Peterson is a lousy liar. She was raised by a gullible grandmother, so it was never something she had to be any good at.

*

Dr. C, wouldn't it be nice if I could pull my life together just for you? I mean, that would be a start, right? Unless, of course, you are troubled by the prospect, by the added pressure this puts on you. Unless it causes you to experience powerful feelings that you are reluctant to acknowledge. At one time or another you shrinks must all feel unequal to the task. Inadequate. How could you not? What sort of creature would you be if you didn't?

★

I know you get over it. I know in the end you feel gallant and good. But really—hour after hour, day after day of doing nothing but talking to us about our feelings. . . . Don't you ever just want to run out and get a gun?

★

Lisa tells Kate, quite rightly, that she may see something in me, but that doesn't mean it's there.

★

It would be nice if I could come up with one of those sweet little insincere invitations, but I can't. Just like I can't call in sick when I'm not, I can't say come on over for dinner or a drink when I really rather you wouldn't.

★

I like the idea of having friends—it's the fact of having them that gives me trouble. In theory they are one thing, in practice another.

★

As I understand it, Carly Brown is what you call a borderline personality. Would you like me to introduce her?

★

There is no method to my madness. I'm worried, and I'm all over the place trying not to be.

*

Sometimes, Dr. C, I wish I wanted to please you more. It would just make everything easier.

*

I have a thing about doctors—you included. I'm always expecting to be told something that I didn't want to know.

*

Peter shook his head. "You know, I'm not worried about this book being cold. That just seems ridiculous to me. If you want something to warm you, get a heater."

*

Can we put the pad away? What if I promise to be cured? It won't be as fast, but it should be as satisfying, you know, to see me come around, get back on the straight and narrow.

*

Aren't you ever afraid of catching something from us—like maybe an overwhelming sense that it is all for nothing?

*

I wonder if anyone has done a study of briefcases and their relationship to personality types. What does Brandon Burdett's saddlebag say about him?

*

Frank Harris is captain of the company softball team. He has a whistle, a clipboard, and a no-nonsense way of putting together a lineup.

★

Who do you see before me? How much of them is still in this room when I get here? How much of them is still in your head? Does X's relationship with his mother ever mix into mine? And who is here after me? What part of my miserable story commingles with theirs? Is that next guy a relief—someone fun, articulate? Someone with a meatier set of problems? Someone who makes the hour just fly by?

★

Jim Maloney always wants to complain about something his ex-wife is doing. An exercise class, a vacation, volunteer work for a would-be state senator—a Republican, for god's sake.

★

I have a feeling that I should want to act like everyone else, but I don't. I mean, I don't care one way or the other—whether I'm acting like everyone else or not. It's just that when I'm not, I find myself wondering why I don't wish I was.

★

Sometimes I think we are working at cross-purposes. I am trying to stop being suspicious of myself, stop suspecting every motive to be ulterior, while you are encouraging me to do just the opposite.

SIX

John Ramsey always comes in here with a magazine.

★

I have never known for sure whether Patrick Mitchell wanted to be director of the Department—if it was something he strove for or if it was something that just sort of came to him as a consequence of having done exceptional work in his previous positions. I am inclined to believe the latter (he just doesn't seem like someone with the patience or finesse to get where he is by political means), but I suspect—as is so often the case in the business world—I'm probably being naive. Once a person hits a certain managerial level he becomes completely incomprehensible to me.

★

It's funny how often I find myself thinking about the place we stayed in Cannon Beach. There's a small patch of unnaturally vivid lawn on which sit picnic tables and barbecues. It's fronted by a short wooden wall that the sand banks up against. It is aged gray and decorated with gull poop. Even on a still day the trees along the adjacent bluff look dramatic, their limbs blown back from the sea and frozen in place. They look caught in some sort of perpetual storm.

★

Kate has a handful of reasonable arguments, but I don't really think they are hers—I think she has borrowed them for the occasion from Lisa.

★

Peter always thought it would be nice to have a father who was a drunken embarrassment. Instead he had an abstemious, angry, petty one who wanted to be a big shot. So, of course, Peter tried to be the opposite—tried to be almost no shot at all.

★

Michelle Sheets shares a cubicle with Jill Kaufman. Largish, exuberant, poorly educated—she was once bitten by a snake.

★

Lucy Braun is in her late forties. She collects dolls.

★

Life is cruel, unfair, and arbitrary. Focusing on the fact does not change it. Neither does ignoring it.

★

I think when Kate leaves me I will plant a tree in her honor—a maple of some sort.

★

There are some things, I'm afraid, that you shouldn't ever feel better about.

*

I don't know where Lisa came up with this guy. Apparently he is someone who knew someone she did, which means—if I know nothing else about him—I know he knows the wrong kind of people. This makes me feel a little better because I trust Kate to pick up on this at some point.

*

Yes, Dr. C, I understand that these days it would probably be considered malpractice not to offer me a prescription. What about a placebo? I might agree to that.

*

Yes, it's possible that I believe I deserve to feel this way much of the time—but I think you should agree that it is possible I am right. Naturally I might want to be consoled, but it doesn't follow that I should be.

*

There are things I know because I know them and things I know because I want to know them. One can feel like the other. Distinguishing between the two is a tricky and tiring business.

*

John Franklin likes to describe himself as having "fled" to this place or that. He likes to think of himself as being involved in some sort of high-speed adventure—as someone pursued for reasons that are ultimately flattering. He is headed for a retreat where he can be coddled and treated as something special, a species of deity—a retreat where he can drink beer and play pool with his fellow deities, a place where they can commiserate with one another.

*

I plan what I will say to Mitchell—thinking if I can say it just so, it will make things different. What is destined to happen won't—something else will, something better.

*

Bacon, eggs, blueberry pancakes, and coffee.

*

Peter gave a reading last night. He acquiesced to the gentle entreaties of Anna King, the owner of the bookstore that had not only stocked, but had featured his book of stories. It was his first reading and, if he's to be believed, his last. He found the experience every bit as unpleasant as he expected. He showed me a generic note he had composed as a response to any possible requests in the future. It reads as follows:

"Thank you for the kind invitation to ———, but because of various other commitments, Mr. Ellis is not available for personal appearances."

*

Kate says the less we discuss this meaningless little dinner, the better. She doesn't want my imagination running away with me. She is probably right, but that doesn't really matter at a time like this.

*

Patrick Mitchell has an unhappy wife, a criminal daughter, and a deranged overweight son. Some here take a certain uncharitable succor in that. They see these significant others as reflections on him, as evidence of fraud, as clear indicators that he is not the faultless, powerful man he likes to present himself as being. While his domestic situation is not likely to be entirely a matter of bad luck, neither is it the sole consequence of his toxic presence. I've met the son (long ago, compulsory function). I doubt after a certain age that PM had much to do with him. Apportioning blame here is a risky business.

★

It's funny what a person will believe if he doesn't care about being consistent.

★

Excerpt from a conversation between Mark Carter and Eric Dillon:

"I don't know what happened—it was like I woke one day and I was a gardener. Soil, air, sun, a trowel, and a watering can—it doesn't seem like enough to make a Saturday, but it is. If you can accept that—well, then, I guess you're about halfway to becoming a Buddhist."

★

If you look closely at the tensions that divide this department into factions you will find that for the most part they have their roots in one or another manager's faith in Patrick Mitchell's plans for us—especially as they relate to the long-term goals of the company. Everyone at a certain level, it seems, has an interpretation of those plans—an interpretation with one thing in common (a central tenet if you will): namely, the belief that however benign, well-intended, or downright impressively imagined another interpretation might be, it is, in the end, tragically flawed and a mortal danger to us all.

*

I don't think I've taken enough tests. There must be something new. I mean "a creative, neurotic, organized loner who finds it easy to be critical"—that's old sausage. Should we make some new? Hasn't something been recently refined? Certainly there is a faster, neater way to get to the bottom of things.

*

What do you make of a man who wants to be a gynecologist? Shouldn't you become one of those by accident? Do you think you can really trust a guy who becomes one intentionally?

*

Cathy Schrader is always telling a story about her delightful little girls—button noses, giggling, nonsense words, dresses worn inside out. Don't you just want to eat them up?

*

Your job, Dr. C—in one way or another it has got to do some terrible things to your view of the human condition. I can't imagine what sort of Latinate game you end up playing with yourself.

*

Stephanie Wright has a face that is all chin.

*

Thank you for the comments, Dr. C. It sounded like you practiced them in front of the mirror this morning. Forgive me if I say I think you are barking up the wrong tree. (Even though I'm afraid saying that will incline you to believe otherwise—unless this was simply an ill-advised test.) It was flattering, but the truth is my ability to forgive myself is second to no one's.

*

What Mitchell doesn't understand (there is no reason he should) is how desperately I am trying to keep my life here from becoming complicated.

*

I don't know who is the greater mystery to me—the sadist or the masochist. I don't find either comprehensible.

*

Bill Marsh is one of those wearing guys who is determined to give everyone the benefit of the doubt.

*

Amy Knight thinks she is as important in your life as she is in her own. She'll talk to you for hours about not feeling smart enough or pretty enough or loved enough or respected enough or valued enough or thin enough or sweet-smelling enough or… enough. It's like an audio lobotomy. Something happens to your brain.

*

I remember myself back then—when I was seven or eight. You wouldn't recognize me.

*

Sometimes, Dr. C, I'm just worn out by it all. I'm tempted to quit, to let someone like you take over, make my decisions for me. It would be a nicer thing to imagine if you guys made fewer mistakes.

*

One person's meaningless little dinner is another person's unanesthetized evisceration.

*

From out in the audience it felt pretty much like a regular reading. Peter introduced himself and thanked everyone for coming. He said that while he was hesitant to characterize the pieces in the book (*Cubicle Dreams*) as "unconventional," he guessed for the most part they were. That didn't mean, he said, they were boring or unreadable—not all of them anyway.

He read a paragraph from "Aaron's Alphabet"—a sort of fractured character sketch—the idea being to sort of orient everyone, to explain his awkwardness at the lectern. Reading was for him, he said, a very private business. He didn't like someone like himself getting in the middle of it. In seeking to do unto others as he would have done unto himself, he would keep it short. He would read a 290-word satire of self-esteem titled "The Manic Mantras."

*

Look at Jay Reed. As a child he was a greedy little cheat. He is the same as an adult. I expect he will thrive. He will sire a tribe of greedy little cheats who we will describe collectively as "go-getters."

*

Dwight Shafer believes certain things are lucky. I asked for an example. He wouldn't give me one. That would be unlucky.

*

Why do the women who ask questions at these things always seem to be wearing capes and berets?

*

No, I have not been tempted to stop therapy. If I had been, I would have reported it. I know you would argue such a wish was symptomatic. The only thing that stands between me and my desire to get better is the insurance company, and so far the wizards in your front office have taken care of that.

*

Jamie Kerr is in her late thirties. She jogs—not because she enjoys it, but because her mother thinks she needs toning.

*

Besides the large square head and steely glower, the thing that makes Patrick Mitchell fearsome is his certainty. He is sure about how he feels. He is sure about how things are. Opinions to the contrary aren't worth wasting time on.

*

Mitchell thinks being a bully is being a man.

*

I have a funny feeling about Lisa. It must have something to do with our mutual dislike of each other, but there are times when I see her that I just want to pick her up by her hair.

*

Sometimes I worry that my frustration might get out of hand,
that I might do something that would actually get me put in jail.
You keep hearing we are becoming more and more litigious as a
society. That makes it harder for people like me—people occasionally on the edge of bad behavior.

*

Swanson's philosophy is "things will work out"; mine is they
won't.

*

Donna Ladish is always talking to us about "just being yourself." It would be nice if maybe once she would be someone else—
like the person who has to listen to one of these little lectures of
hers.

*

It's disorienting to see you waffle, to see you flip back and forth
between those times when you are trying to help me and those
other times when you are trying to study me—between those
times when I am David and those times when I am Data.

*

I wish I cared about being the patient you want me to be. That
would have to improve our chances of making progress.

*

We have to be careful, Dr. C. We don't really know where rev-
elation may lead. The things we discover could make me a better
person—but I think they could just as easily make me a worse
one.

*

Lisa is one of those women who go from one guy to the next with very little space in between.

★

I know to some degree I'm supposed to fall apart in here so that when we put me back together I'm arranged in a better way. But how much am I supposed to fall apart—too much and all we've got is trouble on our hands.

★

Tony Morris is a congenital contrarian. He seems to find arguing fun.

★

Caution, Dr. C. You don't want to get too involved. My failure will break your heart.

★

Melissa Dawkins is always running into things. There are two schools of thought on the subject: she is clumsy or she subconsciously believes she should be punished for something—probably for being Melissa Dawkins.

★

Don Clarkson thinks strange women are always being especially nice to him. It's possible. He is, after all, pretty openly pathetic.

★

I talked with Kate last night. She reported on her experimental date with the experimental Mr. Trotter. It didn't go well at all. He was a gentleman, perfectly nice—but so far as she could tell, she was just more at home with someone like me. In some circles, of course, this will be cause for concern. She said she wasn't going to go into any detail because she knew I was never going to be able to decide how much I really wanted to know.

*

Jeremy Fletcher is a fanatical solver of crossword puzzles. I've tried to admire him, but I can't. Apparently I've missed the point of pointless intellection.

*

Tracy Hamilton has three children—they have all, at one time or another, been bedwetters.

*

If someone shouts at Sherry Laws she will cry.

*

Just because I object to a certain interpretation doesn't mean that it must be right.

*

I have no doubt my view is distorted—maybe even as distorted as yours. So what are we going to do about it?

*

There is something, I would agree. I would also agree that as yet we don't know what—but that the collapse of hope should be looked at as collateral damage? I'd have to say, from my perspective, it is considerably more than that.

*

Excerpt from a conversation between Tim Magnall and Brian Henry:

"I don't know anyone who likes the way their daughter dresses."

         ★

I don't think I hide it very well when I'm talking to someone and start to lose interest. Just watch my face. It's like watching the air go out of a balloon. I try to light up and look focused, but I feel like the crudest bamboozler.

         ★

I ran into the evil manageress this morning. She told me she hadn't gotten my rent check. It's a game we continue to play—a leftover from our old days as sworn enemies. Periodically she will claim not to have received my check. I tell her it was mailed on such and such a day, and she says that she'll have the bookkeeper look into it. She knows Toby and I are staying. She has no intention of making it easy.

         ★

To tell you the truth, there are times when I wouldn't mind taking something that left me in a drooling daze.

         ★

It feels like a winding down. I don't really talk to that many people now, but I've started talking to even fewer. I lose interest in everything. I can't think straight. I have to fight the urge to plop down in my chair and stay there.

         ★

Even if you're right, Dr. C, you shouldn't be. I'm going to try not to listen.

*

Sometimes I don't think I've had enough practice being principled.

*

Sometimes the monotony of good ole common sense can simply flatten you. You can nod yes for just so long before somewhere deep inside you fall asleep.

*

In some ways I've let myself get comfortable. I'm afraid to let it go. I'm afraid I might never be able to get comfortable like this again, and, as a consequence, I'll be made eternally miserable by the memory of what I've lost.

*

Like everyone, if I am worried I might be one thing, I take steps to appear to be another—if to no one else, then at least certainly to myself.

*

Mitchell likes to look tough. It cuts down on the number of times he actually has to be tough.

*

Doesn't it sometimes feel like you are being eaten up by trivialities—like they were ants and you were a sugar cube.

*

I'm constantly amazed by people who think they can tell you anything. They couldn't be more wrong. Nobody can hear anything—not if they're somebody worth telling it to.

*

Lorianne Butterfield's son was attacked by a shark while surfing in Australia.

*

Can one think of himself as forgiving if he is forgiving only up to a point?

*

There is something seductive about the idea of letting go, of being unlatched from a punishing personality.

*

I have images of those endless games of volleyball dancing in my head. Oh, the damaged friends I will make. The hospital gowns I will model. The words I will slur.

SEVEN

I just bought two pairs of shoes—one black, one brown. They were expensive—more expensive than anything I've ever bought before. More expensive by a lot—by almost three times. Somehow, though, I don't feel bad about the money. I'm excited. I'm excited because these aren't just any shoes—these are the shoes that most of the others in my closet have aspired to be. Simple, boxy—they were made in Portugal. They have special soles, special arch supports, and a functionally elegant lacing system that calls attention to itself. They are, for me, the perfect embodiment of an aesthetic ideal.

*

Peter is worried. There was a time when he could have gotten involved in all sorts of serious literary discussion—been as high-minded and polysyllabic as the next guy—but somehow that time seems to have passed. He thinks he might have lost interest in almost every form of argument.

*

Louis Gable has been announcing his anniversary all day—twenty-five years with the company. We are supposed to offer him some sort of congratulations, but it's a hard thing to say with a straight face because to have stayed here for twenty-five years doesn't strike me as something to be proud of. It is brutally boring same-ole-same-ole work—the sort that at some point should cause your brain to leak out of your ears. To do it for twenty-five years suggests a deep-down quivering sort of fearfulness—an aversion to even the most minimal sort of risk. It seems pitiful, not impressive—guarded, not grand.

*

Claudia Vance has been married to three different bankers.

*

My depletion gets on Dr. C's nerves. Why shouldn't it? It gets on my nerves. He's sure the real me is simply hiding, and that that real me is vital and has an extensive repertoire of enthusiasms and interests.

And he accuses *me* of being a romantic.

*

She is someone who can remember telephone conversations from months or even years ago. I can barely remember what I was just saying to Jack Howland, and that was this morning.

*

Kate is not really concerned about my meeting them because she knows this will not have anything to do with the way I think or feel about her. On the other hand, she is worried about them meeting me, about what they will think or feel about me. If it's the wrong thing—as is most likely—they will make life difficult for her in a way only they can.

★

Peter is not an ambitious person. He doesn't think the failure of his book will make him bitter because it's not something he ever expected would succeed.

★

Nancy Brooks is a wearer of many bracelets. She jingles when she walks.

★

If you keep a rat awake for twenty-eight days, it dies.

★

Excerpt from a conversation between Randy Gould and Gerald Hoffman:

"You need to get someone in that house to talk to so you don't end up talking to yourself."

"No. I like it quiet in the morning. Just me and my cup of coffee."

★

"Ideally I would like you to get to a place where you can experience a subtler despair."

There are times when Dr. C simply talks out of both sides of his face—his backpedaling circumlocutions would put a used-car salesman to shame.

★

I just realized what a thoroughly urban animal I've become. I was in the lobby waiting for the elevator when I overheard Art

Cain and Bill Hoke talking about fishing. It sounded so strange to me. I can't remember the last time I heard anyone talk about fishing. It sounded to me like something done in another age—like trapping, butter churning, or plowing.

★

It's a difficult thought to shake—that Kate has brought me here to frighten these people properly, to mobilize them, to leave them no choice but to step in and stop what is going on between us. They would be her easy way out.

★

What is it—a mood disorder, an anxiety issue? Am I looking at depression, a psychotic break, an out-of-control lactose intolerance? Is my view of reality more distorted than yours?

★

Jay Kircher is one of those people who is frequently late, who loses track of time. Peter is envious. He never loses track of time. The hours and minutes—they are always with him.

★

Angie Huffman's four-year-old daughter killed her pet guinea pig, Max. She thought he was cold so she put him in the microwave to warm him up.

★

When you approach the house—a nice two-story thing covered with weathered shingles—you can sense a subtle shift, one that feels something like a dip in barometric pressure. You realize that you have arrived in a place where you are going to be disapproved of. You should be anyway (I would disapprove of me). The thing that changes the dynamic a bit is the degree to which I care about being disapproved of (not that much). The other thing, of course, is how much Kate is going to care. She will care more than me, I am sure, but not so much as to make this moment as important as it would be in a more traditional encounter.

★

When I think about it, I can do this or that or something else. It's the "something else" I can't quite put my finger on.

★

Excerpt from a conversation between Frank Foster and Sean Kramer:

"We've got this strange stain on the carpet near the hall closet. We scrub it with carpet cleaner and it goes away for a week or two, but then it comes back. It's kinda creepy."

★

There are people who have never seen the ocean. That seems to me the deepest sort of deprivation. The ocean and Kate's naked backside—these are the two most beautiful things I've ever seen. I don't know how happy I am (considerably more so than Dr. C thinks)—but however happy it is, I'd be only half if I had never seen one or the other.

★

Lindsey Mattson works in accounting. She has accepted herself. She shouldn't have.

★

Dr. C, what are you like at home? Can you turn it off or have you pigeonholed everyone—your wife, your daughter, your dog?

★

Look at your notes, Dr. C. Where do I begin and you leave off?

★

Mike Nagle starts every week with a "To Do" and a "Not To Do" list. First always on the "To Do" list is "Have a more positive attitude." First on the "Not To Do" list is "Let Marvin Pressinger, Robert Meyers, or Jeff Osborn get to you."

★

Kate suggested I try to keep our conversations short. The more talking I did with them, the greater the chance they would find something they could consider improper. They will do it, she said, because they will want to see how you react when they make it obvious that you have in some way offended their delicate sensibilities. It's one of the ways they go about deciding how much trouble to make for her.

★

Peter was complaining last night about traditional storytelling techniques. He hates the way these guys he has been reading bring new characters on stage—what is his name, who is he . . . say, in relation to the aunt. What does he do for a living, what does he look like (beard? no beard? hair color? eye color?). Where did he come from? Why is he here? It just gets on his nerves sometimes. First A, then B, then C—they gather in the drawing room ready to start behaving novelistically at the drop of a hat.

★

Patrick Dahl is pretty serious about being a Catholic. He has had a difficult life. He was raised on a poor farm in the middle of nowhere. His father was a tyrant. His wife went insane. He assumes at some level we will all feel sorry for him, and, consequently, he seems to expect us all to be generous. He seems neither surprised nor especially grateful for the gifts he receives from strangers. I like him. He is smart and funny—but his sense of entitlement keeps me from liking him more.

★

Have you gotten over feeling strange about the way you see people now—not just people like me, but regular people, people you've focused your x-ray vision on, people who have no idea of what you and your contextual catalogue are doing to them.

★

Connie Meyers loves all board games, but she is especially enamored of Monopoly. She belongs to a group that thinks it's clever to call itself The Mill Creek Proletariat. They play every weekend. They take turns meeting at one another's houses.

★

Don't you think that from time to time you nod at me a little too much?

★

She is short, overweight, round-faced, with brown mid-length hair. I know I'm supposed to have seen her somewhere in the building before. She looks at me like I should know her in some way—but not only is she one of those people who don't make a strong impression, she makes almost no impression at all. I won't notice her again until I see that look—the one that suggests I should in some way recognize her. I try hard not to let on that I haven't the faintest idea who she is, but I think she suspects.

★

Her mother and father will want to know what is going on with us. What can I say—I'm looking for something with Kate. I don't know what it is, but I'm sustained by the possibilities that the looking suggests.

★

Excerpt from a conversation with Peter about his novel:
"There are a lot of things this book isn't going to be. I hope that doesn't get too much in the way of what it is."

★

You get the feeling that Virginia Salvino is one of those women who wants to leave her husband—that she is just waiting for the right time. Whatever it is that is going on with them, it has gone on for a while because there is always something a little wrong with now.

★

Her parents think of her as a reasonable person and she goes along with this to keep them as much out of her way as possible. But she is not that reasonable—that is, not so reasonable as to be thought of as so. If she were, how would you explain me? It is, I know, one of the many things that perplex them right now.

★

Gloria Doyle believes if she exercises more, listens to Mozart, and reads challenging books, she will eventually morph from who she is into who she wants to be.

★

I wish I were here because I had a cough or a runny nose, but I'm not. I'm here because I am alone and insignificant and the chances are that one of these days I'm going to die. I know you can't do anything about that, but it's fun for a while to pretend.

★

Sonya Willner's son is an Elvis impersonator.

★

Excerpt from a conversation with Peter:
"I can only hope the audience for a book like this is larger than I imagine. Otherwise, there is something sad about all of this struggling."

★

It's funny you asked about the future. I don't really have a sense of it—that is, no plans, no dreams—just a vagueness. Mostly I'm just focused on getting through the now. I can't imagine Kate and me in the long term. I can't see much beyond our going out to dinner tomorrow night.

★

Gordon Feeley smokes a pipe.

★

Together we will make excuses for me—and those excuses will make all the difference.

★

Molly Knoll is a pedicureaphile—she is always wearing sandals.

★

Joanne Elliott thinks I look like the actor in that movie she saw three weeks ago but couldn't, at the moment, remember the name of. She is always thinking someone looks like someone else. Ted Doss, for example. She says he looks like Edgar Allen Poe. And Patrick Mitchell—apparently he looks like Benito Mussolini.

★

I don't think there is anything Dexter Evans isn't allergic to.

★

Sometimes Dr. C, a thing just overwhelms me—like the common innocence of a certain smile. It will glow with a significance I can neither specify nor ignore. The simple fact of its existence will paralyze me.

★

Steve Larkin is an aficionado of the detective novel. He reads at least one a week and cannot be compelled to cite a favorite. He thinks the power of even the least of them to enliven a drab life is vastly underrated and that Edmund Wilson should go fuck himself.

★

Wouldn't it be wonderful if there was something we could take for granted—other than confusion, that is?

★

Dave Linden once got kicked in the head by a fireman. He deserved it.

★

I can't award myself credit for giving it a good try. I'll have to leave that to you.

EIGHT

There are times when I no longer know what it is I'm thinking. I mean, sometimes I get caught up in one of those regressive loops—thinking of myself as someone who is thinking of himself thinking of himself. Other times it's just a spooky white noise.

★

I sliced some banana into my cereal this morning. I put in more than I wanted because whatever I didn't use I was going to throw away—a waste that was too blatantly immoral to ignore. I sliced up at least a half. I don't know why because the difference between a third and a half is not enough to relieve the guilt I feel about throwing so much good banana away. I could, I think, throw a quarter away without feeling bad, but that would mean I'd have to put three-quarters of the damned thing on my cereal, which is just way too much. This means what? This means that, as always, I've gotten the day off to a shaky start. I'm barely out of bed and already I've done something wrong, something I will be rationalizing until I can distract myself with something from the newspaper—a story about quake damage in Asia, for instance, or maybe some breathtaking banality from one of the morning shows, something about celebrity haircuts or baby pandas or the amazing things you can do with kiwis.

★

I have a vague leftover idea that other people's fathers are supposed to be a certain type—the sort you would like to pal around with if you were, unlike me, someone who liked to pal around. Kate's father is not this type at all. He's leaner, more ineffectual, less thick-wristed than I expected. Not surprising, however, he wants to talk about the drive—how was it? It was fine until we got stuck behind one of those bloated RVs—one of those two-bedroom houses on wheels that was, as they all seem to be, criminally underpowered, just barely capable of dragging its gigantic ass over the curving ups and downs of the coast range. I had a quiet but vicious fight with myself for thirty or forty miles—tending, as always, to begrudge even the shortest distance between one point and another as a shameful waste of time. It's one of my many problems. Even if I don't want to be where I'm going, I'm in a hurry to get there.

★

Almost everyone except Peter thinks I should have more friends—people with degrees or guitars. His not thinking so is one of the reasons we're so close, I think.

★

This week Dr. C is suggesting some sort of compromise approach to what we are calling my issues. We should be "eclectic." I told him that while I'm frequently in favor of such approaches, in this case it was something I could see right through. It was nothing more than chemistry in reason's clothing.

★

The first thing she asks me to do when I walk in the front door is to ignore the photo of her that's hanging over the piano in the living room. Of course, in asking me to ignore it, she knows I can't. A portrait taken in junior high, it's Kate modeling what is probably the most unintentionally comic hairdo of her life. Filled with air and piled on top of her head, it looks like she is wearing a badly damaged brown balloon. She has asked her parents to take it down she doesn't know how many times, but her father refuses. Like me, he finds her mortification funny.

★

Four people in Hodge's department left to go into real estate. When interest rates went up, two of them returned.

★

There is an obvious tension between Kate and her mother. It is, I think, the standard sort of thing. Kate didn't make much of an effort to hide her feelings because, in addition to being one of those people who like to keep hypocritical expression to a minimum, she is the child and doesn't feel obliged to. Veronica, on the other hand, made the sort of effort you would expect from someone her age and hair-color. She did it for Warren's sake and because she was uncomfortable with her negative reactions, feeling them to be evidence of some sort of personal failure.

★

As apartments go, mine is pretty orderly. There are books, two drippy Kris Hargis paintings, an old oak armoire full of television, an African carving, and Toby.

★

What has happened to your elaborate theory and your rules? Have they been atomized over the years by phalanx after phalanx of obdurate particularity? Are they now just the mist of post-graduate memory? When did your judgment stop and your understanding begin? How have you interpreted the way I seem to be experiencing you? Have I been consigned to column A, column B, or column C? Do we both hear that sound, that echo—not of what I am saying, but of what I am saying is saying?

*

Paul Maynard once touched a porpoise.

*

Peter read something that got him started about a sort of writing he calls the "down-and-outer-than-thou stuff." You know—aren't I colorful, realer than real, tuned in. I haven't shaved, my shirt is bloodstained, you can trust me. You can trust me to tell it like it is because there are cockroaches in my bed. You can trust me because I have lived on beans and radishes.

*

This job should be easily doable. I mean, look at Dr. C's job. At least I'm not having meetings hour after hour, day in and day out, with people like me—or worse. Where does he get the energy?

*

Excerpt from a conversation between Brian Hayes and Charles Market:

"It's not really something she needs—it's just something she wants. She wants it because, I don't know, whatshername has one."

"I don't know how to break this to you, but there is no better reason when you're her age."

"Didn't you ever think if you did things right your kid would be different?"

★

It's a little disconcerting how often the thought of Kate preoccupies me. She appears suddenly from out of nowhere.

★

Dr. C, whatever else happens, please promise me that we will do our best to make sure I don't end up sounding like one of those tedious analysands—you know, one of those people whose idea of table-talk is to drone on endlessly about their boundary issues and their fear of abandonment.

★

Four out of five days Charlotte Price dresses in black. The fifth day she dresses in charcoal gray.

★

We were having chicken. Kate had warned me that Veronica was something of a chef, but that she seemed to have sense enough to take it easy on first-timers. There wouldn't be anything too exotic nor would there be lots of talk about preparation techniques. It would be simple—probably something with one of those girlish spices like rosemary.

★

How long were you doing this before you realized that, in the end, we would not all be grateful to you?

★

Jim Ford lives with his mother. He spends all of his off-hours smoking, drinking, and playing video poker. Everyone wonders how long he can go on like this. Is it a phase or will this, in fact, be his life?

★

Most of the conversation between Kate and Veronica (especially at the beginning) seemed to involve practical matters, things having to do with getting the table set—like where one would find the good napkins or the monkey-pod bowl. Veronica wanted to know if I liked salad. I wasn't quite sure how to answer this because the way she asked it suggested that I should. Since I didn't, saying so wasn't going to be easy—it threatened to get things headed in the wrong direction way too soon. I hedged as best I could by saying "sometimes."

★

Wouldn't it be strange not to come here anymore, not to have to listen to the requests? (I was going to say "ridiculous requests," but they are not—not all of them anyway.) What sort of person would I be if I didn't have to keep putting myself on hold for so much of the day?

★

I don't know what you think happiness is—more than the absence of unhappiness, I'm sure, but what more? I get the feeling your idea of it is a little grand. Mine—what I can understand of it—isn't very grand at all. In fact, it's downright everyday.

★

Kate's sister, Casey, drifts down like smoke from her secret sanctum of suffering upstairs. Tragically tanned and skinny enough to be seen through, she introduces herself as Cass, Kate's divorced sister now living at home with her horrible, but helpful, parents. I shake her bony little hand. I say I'm David, Kate's mentally unbalanced boyfriend—here, I think, to convince her horrible, but helpful, parents that I'm not the nightmare they may have imagined. I'm supposed to help with dinner she says and disappears.

(Kate briefed me on the dissolution of Cass's eighteen-month marriage to Jeremy. I lost interest at the first infidelity, but I faked it to the third.)

★

Yes, I watch you watch me watch you. I want to know what you are doing and why—even though I know it would be better for me if I didn't.

★

Laurie Masters has the look of someone who has waited all weekend by the phone for a call that never came.

★

One of the things I like about him right away is that he really doesn't have any interest in me. He is polite. He will mix in at the dinner table with stories about his first time in an airplane and about growing up on a farm in Iowa. But when the evening is over and we have said our goodbyes, that will be it as far as he is concerned. He won't think about me again—not until I'm back for another meal or his wife brings me up in conversation.

★

There really is no end to the number of ways I can delude myself.

*

Diane Patel doesn't think she knows enough homosexuals. She feels short of chic and would like a few in her weekend club-hopping entourage. It would be all she needed. "You know, someone who would be fun, who would be bitchy about my shoes and my boyfriends."

*

Her mother knows I am seeing a shrink so she assumes, *ipso facto*, that I am a promiscuous user of pills—someone likely to lure her daughter into some sort of psychopharmaceutical misadventure.

*

It's not our relationship that is going to make this work—you're not going to get off so easily. I expect you to know something about me that I don't, and I expect you to tell me what that is—and once you've told me, I expect to be changed for the better.

*

Julie Ladish is married to a model train enthusiast. He is always out in the garage.

*

At dinner we talk about the painting that's hanging over the fireplace—three quasi-abstract women in dark sepulchral gowns standing in some metaphorical relationship to one another in an anomalous interior space. It is good, but out of place. It doesn't go with the general look of the room. It has its decorative elements, but it's too serious. I ask about it. It turns out Kate's mother inherited it. It's from a cousin who killed himself.

★

I'm sure at some point we have all frightened you with our neediness, but who has frightened you the most? What did you learn about yourself from that encounter? What, if anything, have you learned about yourself from me?

★

Excerpt from a conversation between Larry Wilcox and James Mendenhall:
"My daughter wants me to buy her a duck."
"Mine wants me to buy her a car."

★

I know word of me has trickled in over the months from numerous unknowable sources, and it's obvious that Kate's parents were, at first anyway, relieved at the sight of me—having imagined something so much worse.

★

Glen Orloff is obsessed with his lawn. He is forever telling us how he gets it to stay so green.

★

Kate didn't want to be left alone with her mother. She was worried she might say something to her in private, something that would stick in her head. (Apparently there had been relationships in the past that her mother had found unsuitable—not as unsuitable as ours, but unsuitable—and this was the technique employed to put an end to them: a short phrase that devoured your unguarded moments, that stayed with you like some rancid song lyric.)

★

Rick Sandage is not very good about paying his bills. You can hear him on the phone making arrangements with someone to send them such-and-such an amount at the end of the week and another such amount the week after that.

★

There is talk about the father's work (he's an optician), talk about the mother's best friend's daughter who has just gone off to college and is majoring in Music Education, and questions about Kate's job—which they are clearly concerned about. They fear working in close proximity to the mentally ill is danger-ous—there being a chance of someone going berserk and injur-ing people. Trying to put them at ease, I say not to worry—most of the people she has to consort with are just like me: almost never berserk and only once in a blue moon violent. I'm not really amazed that I have said such a thing, but I am caught a little off-guard by the sound of my voice—it's a talking-to-strangers voice I haven't heard in years and suggests to me that, at least momen-tarily, I have drifted further away from the here and now than I suspected. It doesn't sound like me—it sounds like someone else. It's not really a voice I like. Fortunately, I can't describe the look I got from Kate.

★

There has to be at least one of us who has gotten under your skin. Someone you were involved with more than you would like. A "she," I'm sure. Someone charming and suicidal. Someone who enjoyed getting people upset and worried. Someone who made you the doctor you are today—one who can stand there beside himself and watch what he is doing, one who can give himself grades, one who can see that I have annoyed him on purpose and who can use his knowledge of this annoyance to find a way around his counterproductive impulses.

★

As we sit down to eat I look out a pair of large plate-glass windows and notice a storm moving in. The sky is turning steely, and we can hear the fat gray clouds tumbling over one another in the distance. All we need is some music. Something ominous—something filled with shadows and foreboding. The smell of approaching rain is, I suppose, the smell of approaching trouble.

★

With every dollar I spend I become more certain that what we are doing is worthwhile.

★

As I sat there looking at them I wondered what their dreams for Kate had been. One thing I know for certain—someone like me was never part of them. What remains to be seen is how much of a problem this is going to be for everyone.

(My own parents didn't really have dreams for me—none that they shared anyway. I had a feeling they just wanted me to be something rather than nothing, which was the path I seemed to be on.)

★

D!

★

I think sometimes when you understand you should go ahead and judge. Yes, the "why" I did this or that is interesting, but some things simply have to be condemned.

*

You can sense it hovering there above the table—the desire to have a serious talk with me about my future and what I'm planning to do with it. Those questions always make me uncomfortable. I can barely handle thinking about the present.

Did I want some more applesauce? Absolutely.

*

I don't know, Dr. C, I'm a little suspicious of selflessness—those who appear to possess it and certainly those who praise it. If I'm you, I'm glad my neighbor is selfless because every other week I need to borrow his lawn mower.

*

Her parents want to know what I do here. I tell them simply "office work." I don't want to dress it up, try to make it sound important, challenging, or exciting—it isn't. I tell them that the best I can say for what I do is that some of it is occasionally almost necessary.

*

Doesn't it ever frighten you—the tenuousness of identity, I mean?

*

I pray for false impressions—they're so revelatory. Several of them back-to-back—well, that would just be asking too much.

*

I hate luggage. For every piece I have to carry, a certain percentage of pleasure is subtracted from my trip.

*

I have a better idea of what it's supposed to look like than what it's supposed to be.

*

The sort of books Peter seems intent on writing are not likely to make anybody any money. He understands. He can't begrudge a business its desire to remain solvent, but he can complain about an insufficiently nuanced view of profitability.

*

Sometimes you can see clearly what you are doing, but it doesn't help. You just keep right on until it's done and you're sorry about it.

*

It's funny, there are things you are usually able to hide from yourself—then one day whoops, there is that little slip, and you know.

*

Sometimes I think if there is one thing the world doesn't need it's another nay-sayer; other times, I think it's a yea-sayer. What about maybe-sayers—where do they fall in the great scheme of things?

NINE

Clara Stevens is very involved in her church. It seems the congregation is primarily composed of the ailing elderly. Every other week she's off attending a funeral.

★

Nobody knows quite what to make of Tony. He has been married four times, and it looks like it's about to be five.

★

When I leave, my six years of lackluster service will be converted into a defragmented bundle of bits stored on a computer somewhere. The record will contain my name, my address, my employee ID number, the name of my department, notes on my marital status, my hourly pay, my holiday pay, my sick pay, my vacation pay, amounts withheld from that pay by the federal government, amounts withheld by the state government, a list of my charitable contributions, a list of employer-paid benefits. It will sit there unmolested for some prescribed period when it will be deleted to make room for newer data—data relevant to the company's legal obligations. Some here are bothered by this—the completeness of their erasure from the collective memory. They think the company somehow owes them more than what it has already provided. I find I am atypically okay with it. I wouldn't normally expect to face clerical oblivion (or any sort of oblivion for that matter) with equanimity, but in this case I can because as completely as they will forget me, I will forget them. In a few months all that will be left is a small collection of illustrative anecdotes.

★

I've always wondered who Kate imagined she would marry when she was a child. I can't picture him being anything like me.

★

Pam Chappell's daughter is a shoplifter.

★

Wayne Easton owns a rental house. He thinks his tenants are growing marijuana plants in the basement.

★

Sometimes it seems like everything is connected, like there are no coincidences—other times it seems like nothing is, like there are only accidents and chance.

★

Excerpt from a conversation between Rick Hartung and John Cooney:
"I think Tracy might be getting—you know—stranger."
"Like what do you mean?"

"I mean like she thinks I want to know too many people."

"Too many?"

"Yes—too many. She thinks I should want to know maybe three people."

"Really?"

"She thinks I'm distracted. She thinks I should be focused on her and Abbie. She thinks we should be staying home more—that I should be painting the third bedroom and working more in the yard. She has this thing about the Rhododendrons."

★

Bacon, eggs, blueberry pancakes, and coffee.

★

Dr. C, I understand the seductions. Together you, I, and what—maybe half a dozen drug companies—can design a better me. We can adjust my anxiety, my obsessiveness, my gloomy world view. But what does this leave us with a picture of—not a man, but a walking beaker. How many things can we afford not to believe in anymore? You're probably right—we can do away with lots of stuff. A featherless biped who can come up with something like microwave pizza can certainly find a spinnable explanation of this new view—but I'm not sure I've got the strength to ignore what I would have to or pretend what I would have to. I'll grant you, however, that what it may lack in flattering complexity, it more than makes up for in cost effectiveness. I guess what I'm saying is that we should nurture my delusion as opposed to getting me drunk. I mean, ultimately, what is a dose of this or that but a shot of high-tech tequila.

★

There is something about Ted Doss that bothers me. I know you think I should put some time into figuring out just exactly what that something is, but I think it would be a waste. I have no interest in liking him. He is who he is, and there's something about that who I just can't stand. I don't want to know his story. I don't want to give him the benefit of the doubt. What I want is to have as little to do with him as possible.

★

Burst, shrieked, sprang, clutched—Peter is thinking about writing a story full of these overwrought verbs. The idea, he said, is to hide the effete literariness of the thing behind a lot of linguistical arm-waving.

★

Cheryl Hill is married to a lawyer. When they deal with her here it is always by the book.

★

Excerpt from a conversation between Tom Flannery and Bruce Yoder:
"She is faking the senility."
"Why?"
"She thinks if we're afraid she's goofy we won't ask her to stay with the kids this summer."

★

Never sleep with Amanda Fletcher or play poker with John Kindred.

★

Kevin Molina wears his glasses on a lanyard around his neck. If I ever have to wear them I think I'll do the same.

*

I'm not sure what it is, but it is there in the air like a phone call from your internist—something that when heard or realized or understood will put an end to the pleasurable innocence of your plans and prospects, something that will mark the end of the time you will remember as the richest in unequivocal delight—the best time, the time before you heard, before you realized, before you understood. I will try to distract myself because if I can postpone that moment—that moment when I hear, realize, understand—the manageable present will be preserved. But, of course, I can't postpone that moment. That is why I'm here talking to you. I'm hoping you will have something to say. I don't know what. Not something that will make it seem like it didn't happen, like I hadn't heard it, realized it, understood it, but something that will make it seem not necessarily acceptable or as it should be, but as much as possible like any other thing that is.

*

Peter described something he was working on as exhibiting a gilded cynicism that suggested there were quiet moments to fear, but, likewise, similar ones to relish. In short, he said, it's wishy-washy. Like life.

*

I've always thought you guys should wear robes.

*

Nancy Carter is a moviegoer. She smells a little of buttered popcorn. Give her half a chance and she'll ruin anything for you. Her sweaters are always covered with cat hair.

*

One problem with beds is that there is no satisfactory answer to the make-it or don't-make-it question. I grind out a decision every morning, but it's never the right one because the right one doesn't exist—there is only the wrong one. Make the bed, and I feel like I have wasted precious time; don't make it, and I feel slovenly—like someone not brought up right.

*

Kevin Lacy is said to be brilliant—but as he is also basically mute, no one knows for sure.

*

Excerpt of a conversation between Alan Perry and Victor Whittle:

"I don't know why, but I think she is deliberately trying to confuse me. You should see her wander around the kitchen."

*

John Sullivan's review came out on Sunday and Peter was pleasantly surprised. It could have been longer (he measured it with a ruler: 2 ½ inches by 8 ½ inches), but it was nicely situated on the left-hand side of the page with lots of space around it so it stood out. John didn't really express any of his famously tortured opinions, but settled for a lovely and deft distillation of the book's contents. He mentioned the unconventional character of the stories and the author's penchant for first-person narration. All in all—as a piece of naked promotion—it was more than Peter had hoped for.

*

Donald Tower has an incredibly expressive forehead. It's large with a series of wavy lines running across it. These lines are always jumping up and down when he is talking to you. It's very distracting. I'm always having to ask him to repeat something.

*

One thing I can tell you for sure: I'm nobody's first choice.

*

You are charitable about assigning blame—about my degree of responsibility. I'd have to say that, for me, it is your central failing. At the heart of that generosity is an idea that makes me shudder.

*

She is out of town on some sort of business trip, so you go to his place. Are you comfortable there, Miss Collins? Is this really what you want? Why? Are there pictures sitting on the dresser of them on vacation? Don't they look happy? Do you touch something that belongs to her—something other than him? A coat? A comb? A jewelry box? Don't you smell her perfume on the pillow? What is going on? How can people do this to one another?

*

Bruce Ebert thinks his ability to master the newest of electronic gadgets makes him interesting. Actually, it just makes him employable.

*

"Trying to explain why you write is like trying to explain why you laugh—you just do. You're struck by something—you can't help it."

*

Personally, if it had been me, I would have gone into research. I would prefer a little distance from the face-to-face.

★

Ted Doss is one of those people whose shirts and pants are always emphatically creased. The ostentatiousness of this precision suggests quality garments, expensive laundering, and a need to appear error-free.

★

Yes, you listen to me carefully. Sometimes more carefully than you need to.

★

"It's the best thing, I think, that anyone has ever really said to me about something I've written. They said they enjoyed it, but they didn't know why."

★

Mark Strassmaier owns a motorcycle.

★

Excerpt from conversation between Nat Wolfe and Ivan Lindstedt:

"I get the feeling that if it's not messy, she doesn't consider it a relationship."

★

Dawn Ladley is absolutely certain she is going to heaven. She makes Shirley look like a Satan-worshipper.

★

Living together wouldn't be easy. Every time there was a storm she would want me to go up in the attic.

★

Michelle has relatives the way some women have cats—in boggling profusion. I'm never able to keep track of who is who, but then I don't really try. None of them is interesting (except for the fact that at one time or another each seems to have had the quality of their intelligence misjudged).

★

Is art a business? If so, how much is it a business like any other?

★

"I have no idea who my audience might be or what they might expect. I have, for the most part, simply tried to write something I might have wanted to read. In a couple of cases I've come very close to succeeding."

★

You are relentless Dr. C—I'll give you that.

★

I think Peter is too smart to be hopeful or brave.

★

It doesn't seem likely that either of us is going to get what he wants. What we will have, I guess, is a never-ending continuation of the debate. I'm not popping your pills, and you're not going to talk to me about my this and my that. You want something you can measure, something that will make you feel rigorous, rational, worthy of your lab coat. I, on the other hand, want what

I want, which is basically a chance to believe in fundamental things, deluded or not. I want you to hold my hand until I can figure it out for myself. I don't really have much hope that this will happen—my figuring it out. What is more likely is that I'll just get tired of trying, and, as a solution, that will have to do.

★

If I could live a different sort of life, I would be somebody else.

★

I understand scientists can now make a rabbit that glows in the dark.